SECOND CHANCES

SECOND CHANCES

VP Saxton

Library of Congress Control Number:		2019915525
ISBN:	Hardcover	978-1-7960-0550-9
	Softcover	978-1-7960-0549-3
	eBook	978-1-7960-0551-6

Print information available on the last page.

Rev. date: 10/22/2019

To order additional copies of this book, contact:
Xlibris
1-800-455-039
www.Xlibris.com.au
Orders@Xlibris.com.au
780384

CHAPTER 1

PERTH, WESTERN AUSTRALIA, TUESDAY

"So what do you think?" Alan grinned broadly and shoved his hands firmly into his pockets.

Sylvia was making a somewhat vain attempt to prevent the driving rain from running down the inside collar of her raincoat by altering the pitch of her umbrella. "Erm, it's a motorhome, isn't it?"

"Well spotted!" Alan joked, jiggling a small bunch of keys in the air. "Come and look inside." Seemingly oblivious to the inclement weather, he opened the main door of the van and mounted the steps.

After folding and shaking her umbrella, Sylvia followed him in. She looked around the interior. A rigid steel stepladder provided access to what was presumably meant to be a double bed located over the motorised cabin. Some kitchen cupboards, a stovetop, and a sink ran along half the length of one wall. Foam seating covered in bright orange curtain material filled the remaining space at the rear of the van. A small built-in wardrobe stood next to the door, and behind it was a concealed sliding door.

"Wait for it," said Alan, dramatically drawing the door aside to reveal a toilet. "Neat, isn't it?" Alan was still grinning.

Taking in the worn laminate flooring and the faded curtains, Sylvia chose not to comment. "The rain has almost stopped now, and the casserole will be ready. Let's get inside where it's warm, shall we?"

1

Fearing the steps might well be slippery after the rain, she carefully dismounted. Making her way back into the house, she experienced a sinking feeling in her stomach. It had been awhile since Alan had been caught up in a "glitch," as Sylvia referred to his episodes of lack of rationale.

"I thought you'd be far more enthusiastic." Alan was using a spiky green scouring pad to loosen the remaining particles of baked-on chuck steak from the casserole dish.

"Did you?" Sylvia was drying and returning plates and dishes to their rightful places. "I didn't rate the meat much. I'm going to try the butcher next time, rather than the supermarket."

Alan stopped scrubbing and looked at her. "Not about the casserole!" He used his fingernails to scratch off the last few bits. "I meant about the camper van."

"Oh."

While Sylvia had prepared some green vegetables to accompany the meat dish, Alan had busied himself with the post and his emails. He turned on the small TV they kept in the kitchen so they could watch the news as they ate. The TV had been used far more frequently lately.

"I mean when Ben and Suzanne were showing us their photographs last weekend, you were sounding, you know, really keen."

"*Keen?*" Sylvia began drying off the cutlery and sorting it into the drawer.

"Yes. You know, as if you'd like to do the same thing." Alan rinsed the sink.

"Alan, we had been invited around to dinner, and they were full of their recent trip in their—I must say—very grand and new caravan. I was politely sharing in their excitement." Sylvia did not include Alan's brother, Ben, or his wife, Suzanne, on her list of favourite acquaintances. She found Ben patronising and hated the way he used people. Suzanne hardly ever stopped boasting about her three wonderful girls, who were, in fact, beastly to each other and not particularly pleasant to anyone else unless they wanted something.

"But you were admiring the scenery and laughing at the antics of some of the campers."

"Are we missing a serving spoon? That lovely one with the black handle?" Sylvia opened the drawer below. "Ah, here it is." Returning the cutlery item to its station, she closed the drawer with a sense of satisfaction. "A place for everything."

"And everything in its place," Alan mumbled.

WEDNESDAY

The next morning, Alan drove the motorhome around to the back parking lot of the used-car dealership. A motley collection of vehicles, in various stages of disrepair, sadly awaited their fate. Most were given a few weeks' grace before being sold for scrap. Surprisingly, several of them did find new owners. There were always some unfortunate souls battling reduced circumstances and in need of ready cash. Though forced into selling their current means of transport, practicalities necessitated the purchase of a cheaper vehicle. Alan had left his car in the same lot overnight. The dealership was secure and adequately lit. A mobile security firm made regular checks throughout the night.

The car lot at the front of the dealership was altogether more noteworthy. Used cars they may have been, but their polished exteriors and buffed interiors encouraged potential customers to feel that they were purchasing vehicles that would lift their profile and do justice to their rising status. Alan made his way through the double door.

"Good morning, Mr. Meadows," Robert said as he pulled the plug from the vacuum cleaner and cheerfully returned it to its home behind the door marked Staff Only. Alan had grown to like Robert a lot over the short time they had worked together. He was always upbeat and positive, but right now Robert's optimism seemed to add extra weight to Alan's pessimism. "Mr. Big asked to see you at ten o'clock—if it's all right with you." Robert grinned.

"Alan, thank you for finding the time." Ben Meadows gestured to a seat facing his desk while he vacated his own seat and walked across to the expansive windows that fronted the new-car dealership located next door to Alan's humbler place of work. Surveying the dazzling array of glistening brand-new motors, Ben turned his head and smiled at Alan. "I know it's crass, but I think they're beautiful."

Alan was never quite sure how much of his older brother's discourse was deliberately designed to belittle him. Considerably taller than his younger sibling (hence the childhood moniker of "Big Ben," coined by his Cockney father), Ben had worked hard on developing a persona that paid little heed to his early years in London as the son of a market stallholder at Covent Garden. The family relocated to Australia. Both parents worked in and eventually purchased a market garden of their own. Attending a high school in Perth, Ben came to possess an affinity with language. He toned down the rougher edges of his accent yet maintained the charm of apparent working-class sincerity that seemed to win over the majority of clients. Injected Americanisms such as *crass* confused Alan and left him wordless.

There was no doubt his brother had been good to him. On completing a business course at college, Alan had taken an alternate route and had begun to make his name in real estate. He developed a pleasing rapport with clients and made a point of jotting down their particular needs or requirements, memorising them and referring to them often.

At the age of twenty-five, Alan fell hopelessly in love with Nina. She was the most beautiful girl he had ever seen. She worked in the florist shop next to the railway station. A year after they met, when Nina was twenty, he persuaded her to be his wife. Blissfully happy at first, they lived in a small flat, to which Nina lent a slightly bohemian air. As time progressed, Nina became more and more delicate—not so much physically as emotionally. It was as if she were a rare butterfly caught in a net, struggling to be set free. Alan felt he should love her more, but his greater attentiveness seemed to exacerbate the situation. After three years of marriage, Nina left.

Alan fell to pieces completely. His whole world shattered around him. Moving back home with his parents, who were at a loss as to what to do, he earned his keep in the market garden and drank himself into oblivion every night.

"Alan, is there anybody there?" Ben had grown accustomed to what he referred to as Alan's "zombie zones."

"Sorry."

"I said "favourable month," as usual. Kerry gave me the figures." Ben returned to his leather-bound chair and threaded his fingers together as if he were about to pray. "A favour, if I may."

Alan knew what was coming, and it sickened him.

"A new girl, Delvine, is starting tomorrow. If you could, you know, take her under your wing, show her the ropes, I'd be grateful. Paperwork mostly, but see how she gets on with clients. She's a looker, of course." Ben straightened his tie unnecessarily.

Ben had married Suzanne, a good-looking blonde whose most exceptional talent appeared to be spending money. Suzanne had been well trained in this field of expertise by her indulgent parents—their fortunes accumulated through house building and, Alan was inclined to believe, some dodgy deals with one or more of the city councillors. Ben felt entitled to enjoy female companionship whenever it suited. Suzanne either didn't notice or didn't care, so long as she and their three daughters were well maintained. Delvine would be the latest in a long line of devotees. Passing them on to the used-vehicle part of the business meant that, at least for the sake of outward appearances, nothing untoward seemed to be going on. Alan privately referred to these temporary "assistants" as used bicycles. They soon lost their shine.

Walking back to his office, Alan berated himself on several counts. He would always be grateful to Ben for eventually intervening in his sorry state, getting him back on his feet, and providing him with his current job. Nonetheless, did he not owe it to Ben's wife and daughters to remonstrate with him about his lack of moral fibre? Then there were the impracticalities of finding boring and monotonous tasks to occupy the latest conquest without interfering with the daily running of the business. He would need to talk to Robert about handing over some of his functions to Delvine and then being gracious enough to take them back when the lustre wore off and she departed. Also, he was in a stew about the events of last evening. The motorhome couldn't compare to Ben's recent purchase. But he had hoped to open up a bit of a discussion about himself and Sylvia having a few breaks away. All he'd managed to do was alienate Sylvia. It hadn't gone well at all.

CHAPTER 2

"Oh, yes. You've done a fantastic job. I really can't see the repair at all."

Sylvia folded the leather jacket and put it into a bright yellow plastic bag emblazoned with the Hutton's Repairs and Alterations logo and completed the transaction. It sometimes amazed her how much people would pay for alteration, but in this case, the torn pocket on a finely cut jacket had spoilt an expensive garment. The cost of a repair was money well spent.

"Well done, as usual, Sylvia. Another satisfied customer." William deliberately turned his attention towards Crystal, who returned his gaze while continuing to chew doggedly on the bright pink gum that was rolling around in her mouth. "You need to emulate Sylvia, Crystal. She has learnt her trade well and doesn't expect to get away with any slipshod work. And will you get rid of that gum!" William stapled the previous customer's invoice to the job description sheet with unnecessary force. He watched as Crystal slowly got up from her seat in front of the third sewing machine, strolled towards the curtain concealing the small staff area at the back of the service desk, and disappeared behind it. She returned a few seconds later, minus the gum, and picked up her mobile phone.

William appeared to be about to say something but clearly thought better of it. He stood and retrieved his suit jacket from the coat stand in the corner. William was always well dressed. The grey suit he was currently wearing was bespoke and complemented his carefully groomed, still rather boyish, good looks. What he lacked in stature, he made up for in style.

"I shan't be too long, Sylvia. I'm sure you can find a suitable task to engage Crystal."

William walked briskly to the opposite end of the shopping mall. He was pleased to see three potential customers either picking up or dropping off items for dry-cleaning.

Sylvia was the number one seamstress/machinist for Hutton's. As a rule, the business was steady. Ruth, her retired predecessor, could be called in if ever there was a need. William could operate a machine if push came to shove, though he preferred dealing with overall concerns. William was supposedly taking Crystal, his great-niece, under his wing. However, that didn't seem to be working too well.

Mounted on the rear wall at the back of the workshop, a range of shelves and compartments held all the accoutrements and necessities for them to ply their trade. One compartment was reserved for Sylvia. Knowing she had soon become highly valued by William, she negotiated the right to work on her pieces whenever all current jobs were up to date. After all, busy staff made for a good impression, she reasoned. Regularly scouring second-hand stores for items that inspired her imagination, Sylvia would unpick, remake, restyle, and revamp to create one-off masterpieces, sold via the market stall of Vivienne, her good friend. They commanded a fair price too, and occasionally she might get a commission. Alterations and repairs provided the bread and butter. Creating quality garments was the icing on the cake.

Sylvia handed Crystal a pleated full-length skirt that swirled with purples and pinks. "Would you unpick this for me, please, Crystal?"

"Sure. Beats replacin' zips."

William greeted the dry-cleaning staff and went straight through to the small office at the rear of the store. A three-drawer filing cabinet constituted the hub of his business empire. There was a lock in the top right-hand corner of the unit. The top drawer held all things related to Hutton's Repairs and Alterations, along with Hutton's Dry-Cleaning Agency. The suspension files had been pulled forward to allow room at the back of the drawer for a good bottle of Scotch and two glasses.

The middle drawer dealt with matters relative to the two units he owned. Both were in good locations. William lived in the smallest, passed on to him by his paternal grandparents when he was quite young, along with an old-fashioned tailor shop. The area underwent drastic changes in the nineties. Roads were closed, shopping malls erected, and arcades knocked through. William was well compensated for the loss of his business premises. He promptly opened up the dry-cleaning agency as well as the repair shop in the Brightwater Mall. As soon as a flat became available in one of the more desirable residential developments, he purchased it and rented it out.

The bottom drawer revealed documents pertinent to two cars. One was William's regular vehicle. The second was hired out for special occasions or used to pick up visiting business associates, transferring them to and from the airport, casino, or hotel. More often than not, William chauffeured it. He prided himself on knowing how to be discreet. He had found, of late, that there were more of these trips than he liked to fulfil. Rather than turn down business, an advertisement in the local paper had resulted in the employment of a pleasant young man, paid directly per kilometre, to take William's place when he wasn't in the mood.

William sat down at his desk and opened his extensive business diary. A computer stood idle. The agency staff used a computerised system for dealing with the service provision, but William preferred working with pen and paper. To this end, he picked up the phone and made a call.

Alan found himself in the unenviable position of trying to explain to Robert what would need to happen regarding Delvine. "It's not my place to ask, but is there enough work for another staff member?"

Robert's mobile rang. "Sorry. Do you mind if I take this?"

"Go ahead." Alan was quite pleased with the distraction.

Robert took the call outside and returned a short while later. He had been checking the ownership details on a recently purchased vehicle. Picking up the pen, he tapped the counter a few times, as if deep in thought, coughed, took a breath, and then appeared to be absorbed in the paperwork once again.

"No. You're right. There isn't enough work to justify another staff member."

"Mr. Meadows, I know I've only been here a short time, but I think I've proved my worth. I've tried—"

"Yes. Of course, Robert. No question. Your job is safe."

Robert nodded and walked across to the coffee machine. "Can I get you one?" Alan nodded gratefully. Robert had a good head on his shoulders and seemed to know how to handle people. He played cricket for a local A-grade side and coached an underage team. Reassured that his job did not appear to be in jeopardy, he ploughed on.

"Well then, I hope I'm not speaking out of turn, but as you know, professional cricket is a long-term goal for me. I also happen to like cars. One day, when I'm too old to play for Australia," he added, not entirely tongue- in-cheek, "I want to sell people nice cars. I appreciate Mr. Big ... Sorry." He grinned. "Your brother giving me this opportunity,"

"He has some fine qualities ..."

"Sure does. But he likes women, right?"

Alan shifted uncomfortably in his seat.

"And he's married. Right?"

"Right." Alan gazed out of the window.

"So promising a job is part of the deal, right?"

Alan was unprepared for this level of honest communication.

"He hopes that before long they get fed up and sod off. Right?"

"Robert ..."

"Tell me if I'm wrong—just don't sack me!"

Alan was astounded. There was no malice whatsoever in Robert's explanation of events. He was merely stating facts.

"The thing is," continued Robert as he handed a coffee to Alan and took a sip of his own, "he's the boss."

"Right." Alan ran his finger around the edge of the coffee cup.

"Now. Here's another thing. I sometimes do a bit of moonlighting."

"What do you mean?" Alan wasn't familiar with the term.

"Some nights I do a bit of driving. I know this chap who owns two nice cars. He sometimes needs a chauffeur to take people places. I like driving nice cars. I get paid. Everybody wins."

"Good for you. That doesn't affect your job here, though, does it?"

"No. But he has just phoned to ask if I'd be willing to do the occasional daytime drive. I told him I'd think about it. I didn't want to knock it on the head straight off, but if we've got an extra staff member, where's the harm?"

Alan concentrated on his coffee. Ethically, he should probably say no. Ben was paying Robert, after all. But both he and Robert were placed in the awkward position of pretence.

"What do you know about this *chap*?" They both watched as a car was driven into the lot and parked in one of the designated bays. Robert went out through the double doors immediately to greet the potential customer. His ready smile and helpful manner won people over quickly. Since he had joined the firm, most of the sales had been down to him, to be honest.

Robert was following the usual routine of asking whether the customer was looking for a straight trade or a trade-in. The two of them would often have a quiet punt between themselves as to which car they would go for. Alan watched as Robert led the gentleman towards the two best 4x4s they had on their books. He felt confident in his prediction of his selecting the later model.

Alan's thoughts returned to the situation of Delvine and her imminent arrival in the morning. Ben did have a bloody cheek. To take his mind off the problem for a while, he decided to check out the competition of his local rivals on the net. They weren't rivals in the real sense of the word. When Robert came back in with the prospective buyer to collect the keys for a test drive, Alan decided that the decision was his to make; and as long as the business came first, no harm should come of Robert occasionally moonlighting.

Driving his usual car home that evening, Alan was debating in his head as to whether it was better not to mention the camper van at all or apologise for having a dumb idea. Realising that he had "spooked" Sylvia, he might suggest going out for dinner as a sort of peace offering. Maybe it would be best not to mention the van. After all, it didn't conjure up images of the two of them setting off excitedly for a little weekend adventure. Sylvia's imagined presence was blotted out by someone else entirely.

CHAPTER 3

Sylvia bought an appetising piece of barramundi from the fishmongers on the way home. She and Alan had exchanged very few words after dinner yesterday and had tiptoed gingerly around each other this morning. Alan was caring and thought a lot of her, she knew, but somehow something was missing. The incident with the camper van would have been funny if it had happened to someone else. Alan, however, seemed comically tragic when he came up with these hare-brained ideas. Hopefully, the van would have been returned and forgotten. Tonight she would be more pleasant.

Having assigned the food items she had purchased to the fridge, Sylvia added a little milk to the strong tea steeping in a delicate blue mug with hand-drawn pictures of shoes on it. She owned a set of three, discovered in an arty gift shop about a year ago. The remaining two were pink with handbags and yellow with hats, respectively. Discarding the teabag, she picked up the mug carefully, collected her work tote in her other hand, and carried both through to the sitting room, where she kept her laptop. The familiar ringtone from her phone alerted her, but by the time she reached the gate-legged table that served as both dining area when guests were present and a study desk at most other times, her mobile gave up. Spilling a little of her tea as she placed both

13

cup and bag on the tabletop, Sylvia grabbed a tissue and wiped the spill before searching for her mobile.

It had been Vivienne. Sylvia was surprised, as she usually spoke to her friend regularly on a Thursday evening. Two missed calls. Something must be up.

"Sylvia. Thanks for ..." Sylvia heard a crack in Vivienne's voice, followed by a forced breath.

"What is it, Viv? What's happened?"

"It's Bibi and Joe, Sylvia."

Pulling out a cushioned chair from beneath the table, Sylvia sat down. "I'm listening," she said. "Tell me."

Sylvia breathed a sigh of relief upon hearing the familiar sound of Alan's car. When he walked in, she was retrieving the fish from the fridge and foraging in the bottom drawer for new potatoes and green beans. She could immediately tell that Alan was over the "glitch."

"Have you started on dinner yet?" Alan quickly crossed the floor to where she stood, smiled brightly, and kissed her firmly on the cheek. "I thought we might go out."

"Oh. That would be a nice idea, but ..."

Alan recognised the usual paper wrapping that accompanied fresh fish.

"But you've bought fish? That's nice too. We could have fish tomorrow. Shall we go out?" Alan was hoping for a returned smile at least.

"Alan, I'm sorry, but I don't feel like going out. It's just ..." Sylvia bit her lip and laid the ingredients out on the worktop. "It's just ..."

Alan put his arms around her. "It's just what?"

"I've had bad news." Sylvia returned the embrace. They hugged for what seemed like ages. Eventually, Sylvia broke away from him and located the box of tissues on top of the fridge. She pulled out several and covered her face with them. She dabbed at her eyes and cheeks, knowing there would be more tears.

Alan filled the kettle. "How about I make dinner while you tell me everything?"

Joe and Barbara, or Bibi, as she was known for as long as anyone could remember, were grandparents to Vivienne and her brother, Tom. Between them, they virtually raised their two grandchildren, enabling their son, Peter, and his wife, Meg, to put their heart and soul into a travel business that often took them away from home. There was very little thought or discussion over the arrangements, as everything seemed to tick along nicely. One large house, situated in central London, served everyone well. People came and went amid the clutter and the chatter and happily coexisted.

Sylvia and her mother had lived next door in a small ground-floor flat. Money was short. Her father seemed to come and go at will, while her mother eked out a living as a seamstress. Sylvia soon became a somewhat unofficially adopted member of her neighbours' somewhat haphazard household, spending more time there than at home.

Sylvia thanked Alan for the tea, made for her in the yellow mug. She had splashed her face in the bathroom and tidied her hair after blurting out to Alan that it was Bibi and Joe, but she had said no more. She took a sip of hot tea and smiled. At times like this, Alan was simply lovely. She liked watching him cook. He was able to deftly go about the business of putting a well-constructed meal on the table and hold a thoughtful conversation at the same time. That was when he appeared his most attractive to her.

"Apparently, Bibi and Joe had been shopping for the day, for bathroom accessories, of all things." Sylvia shook her head as if disbelieving. "They travelled into town by bus because it is free between eleven in the morning and two in the afternoon." Sylvia rolled her eyes. "Returning with several large bags between them, they stood up on the bus journey home because of the awkward loads. Joe completely lost his footing when he got off. He tumbled right over and hit his head hard on the kerb. Bibi saw it all, and—typical Bibi—she rushed to help and tripped over all the bags, spraining her ankle." Sylvia took another sip of tea and then gave in to more tears.

"Presumably an ambulance was called." Alan wasn't going to voice the fears in his head.

Sylvia nodded and then grabbed more tissues. "He died, Alan. On the way to the hospital. He just died."

Alan turned off the TV news. He had suggested that Sylvia go and lie down for a while, assuring her that he would be there if she wanted to talk or be with someone. They had met when Sylvia had needed to purchase a vehicle. Ben had scored tickets to a movie as part of a sales promotion and given them to Alan. As they chatted amiably over the paperwork, Alan and Sylvia discovered a shared liking for foreign films. A date resulted. Alan thought Sylvia was admirable in many ways. She wasn't Nina, though. He knew it wasn't fair, but Nina was, well, Nina. No one else would ever come close.

Sylvia woke suddenly and looked at the clock. It was eight at night by then. Sadness flooded over her again. She should go spend some time with Alan. Life was bloody awful sometimes.

"Tell me about your day," Sylvia said as she came through into the kitchen. "Good or bad?"

"Neither, really." Alan didn't usually have too much to say about work. "Figures are all good according to Ben. He's back to his usual tricks, of course. Another of his fancy pieces starting tomorrow."

"You make yourself sound so old fashioned! His fancy piece." Sylvia laughed. "It's awful, though. I'm sure Suzanne must know about his … dalliances."

"Now you sound old-fashioned!" Alan seemed pleased to see Sylvia smile. "Do you think she knows? Why would she put up with it?"

"Well, from what I've seen, she enjoys an enviable lifestyle. House, location, holidays, spoilt brats … Sorry, I mean overindulged children." Sylvia hesitated for a moment. "It's not always about love, is it?" Sylvia avoided Alan's eyes and retrieved a tissue from her pocket.

Alan picked up the newspaper and then spoke. "Oh, I meant to ask: does your boss do car rentals?"

"William? Yes, I think so. Why?"

"I think Robert drives for him sometimes. He asked today if he could occasionally do a day run. My first reaction was no way, but if he has extra time on his hands … Mind you, he is a good salesman. Perhaps I should wait and see how things pan out with … what's-her-name, Delilah?" Alan snorted at his witticism.

"Alan," Sylvia interjected, making for the door. "I need to go to bed. Sorry. Thanks, though."

Alan returned to the newspaper and located the horoscope page. He had no belief in horoscopes whatsoever. However, an astrologer coincidentally named Nina wrote the column. He read it almost every day. He couldn't explain, even to himself, why this exercise gave him a measure of comfort. He removed the throw blanket from the sitting room sofa, wrapped it around himself, and curled up on the cushions. He was asleep within minutes.

CHAPTER 4

Suzanne watched twelve-year-old Jade saunter along the pathway towards the main school building. On seeing Sophie, she waved, and they fell in step together. Sophie Donaldson was the daughter of Eric, a local member of Parliament, tipped eventually to wind up in the cabinet or some such. Suzanne wasn't sure how that all worked, but anyway, he was somebody. Jade had invited Sophie along to her birthday party two weeks ago. A party hire company erected a marquee in the garden, a DJ was engaged, and kiddie party food provided by caterers. Suzanne had considered the kiddie treats a stroke of genius after overhearing Dr. Robson's wife complaining to a group of fundraising mothers that "children weren't allowed to be children for nearly long enough nowadays."

"Mum, the top keeps falling off of my tower. *Doooon't!*" Opal yelled at Pearl, who was poking her fingers into the widening gap between the beautifully painted toilet roll cylinder and its impressive domed rooftop.

"It's not a tower, Opal; it's a minaret. Don't poke it, Pearl. Your dad spent ages doing that. I'll fix it in the car park. I've got some sticky tape."

"I want the Jiggles. Mum, I want the Jiggles on. *Mum!*"

"I hate the Jiggles. They're stupid. You're stupid!"

"Mum, Opal said I'm stupid!"

"Stop it, both of you. We're nearly at the car park." Suzanne was thankful that both schools were within a few minutes' drive of each other. She pulled up on the grass. (Strictly speaking, it wasn't allowed, but this was an emergency.) Removing the tape from her bag, she hurriedly stuck the offending segments together. The two girls lagged after her as she carried the multicultural appreciation project to the classroom herself. The precarious minaret was knocked out of place as mother and daughter bade a speedy farewell. Opal's classroom teacher, Mrs. Bender, came to the rescue with more tape. She clearly had a soft spot for Suzanne, whose whole life appeared to be held together with sticky tape.

"Thank you so much." Suzanne smiled gratefully and looked around the classroom for Pearl, who had disappeared under one of the tables in search of some glitter stubbornly adhering to the carpet. "Come along, Pearl, please."

"I've got some glitter to take home." Mrs. Bender watched as Suzanne dragged Pearl from underneath the table and out of the room. Pearl's protestations over the acquisition of the glitter could be heard plainly above the din of parents and children. Suzanne hastily made her way back to the car before anyone had a chance to tell her she shouldn't be parking on the verge.

The drive home wasn't lengthy, but it offered the chance to breathe and think. Sophie belonged to the pony club. Jade wanted to join the pony club. More to the point, Jade wanted a pony. It was perfectly understandable. She had collected Precious Pony toys when she was little. Suzanne felt that joining the pony club was practically a requirement if she wanted to remain friends with Sophie. Sophie had performed very well at the Gymkhana. Ben, however, had spoken quite sharply when she broached the subject last evening. He even said it wasn't up for discussion, which wasn't like him at all. Mind you, he was a bit stressed over the multicultural appreciation project. She racked her brain, trying to think of one of his dinner favourites that she hadn't cooked in a while.

Three days a week, Suzanne scrubbed the whole house virtually within an inch of its life. Anything to do with laundering would be taken care of on Mondays and Fridays. Midweek the patio area was swept and dusted, the plants tended and nurtured, the food shopping purchased and packed neatly away. Prince accepted that his place of residence was strictly limited to the garden and patio, but seeing as Ben took him to the park almost every day for a walk, chase, and play, he felt reasonably well treated on the whole.

Would salmon suffice for tonight, perhaps? Maybe she would feed the girls early, leaving her and Ben to have dinner on their own. Or would he see through that? Broaching the subject of a pony over coffee would be difficult.

Considering her options and admiring her domestic handiwork, she found herself in front of the computer. Very little money remained in her clothing allowance—or the girls' clothing allowances, for that matter. And the Christmas fund? There were several months to go before Christmas. Wouldn't it be wonderful if she could come up with the money for the pony club fees herself? If Jade became a member of the pony club first, it would naturally follow that she would need a pony eventually.

Suzanne turned on the computer.

"Good morning. I'm Robert, and you must be Delvine." Robert offered his hand.

"Pleased to meet you." Delvine smiled, returning the handshake.

Robert was shocked to encounter Delvine waiting by the reception entrance the next morning. He was also a little taken aback by her appearance. She wore a smart pair of black pants paired with a matching jacket over a pale pink shirt, unbuttoned at the collar to add a discreet feminine touch. Her light brown shoulder-length hair was pulled back above her ears and fastened with a large clip, allowing the rest of it to hang naturally.

"I'm sorry to have kept you waiting. I'm normally here by around eight thirty. Mr. Meadows arrives a bit later."

"That's okay. The next bus would have gotten me here at about five to nine, so it was cutting it a bit fine."

Robert nodded in agreement, wondering if there had been some mistake. Expecting to see a brassy blonde in a short skirt, stiletto heels, and enough make-up to sink a battleship, he certainly wasn't expecting a well-dressed professional-looking young woman travelling by bus. Directing her to the staffroom, Robert immediately felt a slight sense of embarrassment. A higgledy-piggledy arrangement of office paraphernalia, along with various bits of furniture, a vacuum cleaner, and some cleaning equipment in a bucket forlornly lined the walls. A coatrack consisting of four pegs completed the staff facilities.

"The place gets cleaned once a week. The first job every morning, though, is to vacuum through." Robert shifted a little uneasily on his feet.

"Of course." Delvine eyed the (thankfully) relatively recent vacuum model. "Erm … is there a loo? Then I'll start on the vacuuming." Delvine looked around and placed her generously sized bag beneath the coatrack.

"Oh, yes. Over on the other side. Staff shares the disabled one, I'm afraid." Robert pointed across the office floor, where a sign on the wall indicated restrooms. Robert was also supposed to delegate the morning loo clean to Delvine. He thought maybe he'd hang on for a while. "There is also a small kitchen; it's behind the service desk."

"Thank you." Delvine removed a small bag from the larger one and headed across the floor towards the restrooms, which were actually located along a corridor and around to the back of the building, offering privacy. There was even a shower cubicle.

Alan walked into the reception area to find a rather nonplussed-looking Robert standing behind the desk, busying himself with some paperwork. Delvine appeared from the corridor and approached Alan directly with her hand outstretched.

"Good Morning, Mr. Meadows. I'm Delvine Raft. I'm very pleased to meet you."

Alan took in the way she looked and stammered a reply. Both he and Robert watched as she went into the staffroom to collect the vacuum cleaner.

"Well, I need to see Nev in the workshop. I'll leave you both to it, then."

All the used vehicles in Alan's car yard would be handed over to Nev. Nev, assisted by his brothers, Shane and Des, ran a repair shop. They ensured the cars were roadworthy and as presentable as possible. Of course, the cost of any work they did was added to the asking price. Any hopeless cases were transferred directly to the scrapyard, which also turned in a profit for Nev and company. His mother, Aileen, did the books and kept the boys in line. Her husband, Raymond, worked for the Aboriginal Legal Services and often brought home a stray who would live and work with them for a while until they got on their feet. Alan thought the whole family deserved the Australian of the Year Award.

Shane and the family's current "work experience" lad, who went by the somewhat unique name of Schubert, were at the rear of the property, filling in logs and discussing the latest round of vehicles and their potential. The last one on the list was the camper van.

"Haven't seen one of them in a long time. Can't see it selling. Not from here anyway." Shane was usually right. He knew what would sell quickly and what would hang around.

"If you'd just make sure it runs okay ..." Alan didn't want to see it go. Not yet anyway.

"Right, boss," said a surprised Shane. "We'll get this lot back, then."

Sylvia was colour matching a bridesmaid's dress with thread when Crystal ambled in unenthusiastically.

"What a revolting colour. Who'd have bright green bridesmaids?"

Sylvia privately thought the colour garish. However, she did not comment. "Crystal, I'm going to be asking for some time off to attend a funeral. I have to go to England, so I'm hoping to persuade William to allow me some extra leave. If you play your cards right, this could be a golden opportunity for you." Crystal blew a large bubble of gum and allowed it to pop. You could win William's respect for your talents if you work well with Ruth, and I'm sure he will encourage your mum to think about a course in fashion design. We all have to prove our worth first."

"What—replacin' zips and mendin' pockets?"

"Show him you're capable of hard work. You get nowhere without working at it, Crystal."

"Can I do some of your special stuff while you're away?"

"No," Sylvia replied firmly. She saw William approaching and adopted what she hoped was a suppliant air.

"Sylvia wants a month off," Crystal blurted out as soon as William was within earshot, making a big show of taking down a skirt from her allocated pile of repairs. Sylvia shot her a glance that could have killed at twenty paces.

"What's this, Sylvia?" William arched his neat and tidy brows.

"Could we have a little chat, please, William?" Sylvia left her chair and walked through to the back room.

When Sylvia emerged fifteen minutes later, they had settled on an agreement. William extended the seven days of remaining holiday leave to ten, including sick pay. Three days would be unpaid, starting the following Monday. Sylvia picked up one of the company bags. Slowly and deliberately, she folded her potential designer garments into the bag and placed them under her machine desk. Crystal blew another giant bubble. It burst unexpectedly and left her with gum all over her silly face.

"I can help with the fare if you need it. Thing is, they tend to slug you when it's short notice, don't they?" Alan was frying a little bacon to add to the scrambled eggs they had settled on for tea.

"Thank you." Sylvia circled her arms around his waist. "You are a good man, Alan Meadows. But I have some savings. I'm sorry about the last few days. The camper van—"

"No. Don't." Alan stirred the bacon into the eggs, topped the toast with the mixture, and ground some pepper over both serves. "I'm sorry. I can't explain."

"Some ghosts refuse to lay to rest, don't they?" Sylvia took the plate. Thank you for this." Smiling at each other, they took the plates to the table and sat down to eat. "You could come with me."

"No, thank you. First, it's twice the cost. Second, don't feel happy about leaving the office at the moment. Third, you need to do this for you—lay some of your own ghosts to rest!"

"Me? Ghosts? What ghosts?" Sylvia's phone rang. It was Vivienne. The ensuing conversation was brief and ended with Sylvia brushing away tears.

"Viv. She phoned to say she booked the tickets, and …" Sylvia grabbed a tissue and dabbed at her nose and eyes. "And she insists on paying. I fly on Saturday."

"Better go pack, then," said Alan. "Finish your eggs first, though."

CHAPTER 5

Delvine had exchanged both the black pants and pink shirt for grey on Friday morning. She brought in a hanger to accommodate her jacket more satisfactorily and had procured a large basket, probably used as the receptacle for a gourmet hamper at one time, placing it beneath the coatrack to provide a home for her bag. She opted to clean the loos before she vacuumed the floors, and she suggested that the cleaning items. could be stored in the unused shower recess. Robert and Alan thought it a brilliant idea and didn't know why they hadn't considered it before. Once she had relocated the cleaning items, Delvine swapped her flat shoes for heeled but comfortable sling-backs.

"Our staffroom does leave a lot to be desired. Robert and I were saying that only the other day," Alan lied, looking at Robert expectantly. Robert nodded in silent agreement.

"I shouldn't ask, as it's not your job, strictly speaking, but if you'd like to take a pad and paper in there, have a think, and make some notes on how it could be improved, I'd be willing to raid the 'fixture and fittings' budget—well, some of it. There's an office equipment catalogue behind the desk somewhere." Robert hastily went in search of the flier and was grateful for its attention-grabbing cover page. "I'm not making wild promises, though!" Alan laughed, seemingly unable to decide quite what he wanted. "Oh. Potential customer!" Alan eagerly left the office and made for the car lot.

Robert handed Delvine a pad, pen, and the brochure and enthusiastically joined Alan outside. Their surprised new staff member was left to get on with the task

Ben was once again reliving the events of a few days ago. He had returned from work, greeting everyone as usual. Suzanne was busy in the kitchen. She cooked well; he acknowledged that—efficiency served on a plate. The table looked attractive, as did she. But it wasn't done for him, not really. He could hear the girls arguing about a television program as he showered and changed into a tracksuit, ready to take the dog to the park.

Prince bounded after the ball that Ben kept throwing for him. He was amused and delighted by the unashamed abandonment shown by the family pet he had rescued from the pound a few years ago. Ben picked up the ball dropped at his feet and, without looking, threw it hard towards the dense shrubbery growing behind three wooden park benches several metres away. Horrified, he watched as the ball flew through the air and hit a young woman who was sitting on the central bench squarely on the shoulder. She sat bolt upright, seeming totally shocked to see both Ben and a most excited dog hurtling towards her.

"My God," Ben sputtered. "I'm so sorry. I can't believe I wasn't looking. I'm such an idiot." As he drew closer, Ben saw the girl's face. It was red, blotchy, and tearstained. She must be hurt. Oh God, he didn't know what to say. He watched as she picked up the ball and handed it back to him. "You're hurt! I'm so dreadfully sorry."

"It did hurt, to be honest. I'll have a bruise, but I'm okay." She rubbed her shoulder. "I think so, anyway."

"It must have hurt—it made you cry."

"Oh, no." She brushed her hands hastily over her face. "Your dog wants to play. And I must go." She rummaged in her bag for a tissue, wiped her eyes, and made to leave.

"Please stay a little bit longer. I feel so bad about this. You might have a concussion."

"I didn't hit my head!" She laughed, but she winced and rubbed her shoulder again.

"Just five minutes. Sit down for five minutes."

Ben's recollections were interrupted by a knock on the door. He had asked Mrs. Lancer to show Enrique Castro through on arrival. He was there to discuss a lucrative corporate deal.

Suzanne felt sick. Ben didn't have too much to do with the organisation of their domestic money dealings. He managed all the finance related to the business and paid a generous allowance into a family account for Suzanne to handle as she saw fit. He had no reason to question her ability in this area. They ate well; the house was tastefully furnished and always looked immaculate. The children and Suzanne were well dressed. When he wanted to update his wardrobe, the money was there. They had grown accustomed to a ten-day family holiday abroad every year, until recently, when Ben had taken advantage of an excellent deal involving a state-of-the-art caravan. Suzanne had felt that the caravanning experience would be perfect for the girls. It would "build up their sense of resilience, encourage independence, and promote a healthy lifestyle." Well, that was the view of the national representative for YEHA (Youth Experiencing Healthy Attitudes), whom she had heard address the CPG (Concerned Parent Group) last year. In all fairness, the talk was focussing on the advantages of camping under canvas rather than luxury caravanning. Sleeping rough, however, as Suzanne described it, was not an option.

Nausea overcame her, and she rushed into the bathroom. Taking some deep, steady breaths, she managed to calm herself. Her nausea gradually eased. She couldn't account for how this had happened. Well, she could. It had happened as she gradually transferred money into the SafeBet site. Conscious of the Please Gamble Responsibly caution at the bottom of the page, she only wagered ten dollars at a time. Ten dollars was nothing, right? Why did it add up so quickly? The Christmas account, now completely depleted, certainly didn't offer up much joy, seasonal or otherwise. There were quite a few months to go before Christmas, though. She could recoup the loss and no one would be any the wiser.

"Thank you so much, Ruth, for standing in. You're brilliant. I mean it." Sylvia hugged her warmly.

"To be honest, although I'm sorry for the circumstances, I was thrilled that you asked. Everyone tells you retirement is wonderful, but I'm bored silly."

"Well, I had hoped to clear everything before you came in, but someone has dropped off this huge consignment of curtain alterations. The customer loves the fabric design, and the colour is perfect, but she wants a particular swathed look. She's taken an illustration from a home magazine."

"Very classy. It'll cost a small fortune. But I'll enjoy having something to get my teeth into. Sylvia, don't worry about those small orders. I'll get Crystal cracking on those on Monday morning."

"Good luck with that!" Sylvia mimicked chewing gum. Crystal had gone off to the loo.

"Oh, she's not so bad. I'll pull the grandmother angle. She'll be putty in my hands! Why don't you get off? Your mind must be all over the place. I'll square it with William if he comes back. Go on. Concentrate on your packing."

Geoffrey and Martin loved their flat. It had quickly become home to them both, and it was large enough to house a piano. Geoffrey, however, was gradually becoming uncomfortable with William as a landlord. Not long after they had moved in, William had called in to say how sorry he was for the inconvenience, but there was a clause in the local council fees that he had been unaware of, and he would have to charge an extra two hundred dollars a month to cover it. He would be happy for a regular cash payment to be made, rather than going to the trouble of redrafting an entirely new rental agreement.

Martin was reasonably philosophical about the regular extra payment to William. He maintained that they should have refused to pay the bogus fee from the outset and asked for the shire bill to be sent to them directly. Now it was too late. Besides, another flat in the same area would cost them more anyway.

Geoffrey was incensed. He knew they were being blackmailed because they were gay. Yes, of course, many no longer perceived it as problematic. When the partners in question were a doctor and an educator, however, it wasn't quite that simple. Not wanting to cause ill feeling with Martin, he continued to go along with the distasteful charade. One day William would get his comeuppance.

Both Geoffrey and Martin were involved in their local amateur theatre company, Opening Act. Geoffrey worked on sets and played the piano when required. Martin occasionally acted, but more often than not, he directed their productions. His artistry with make-up was well renowned. The theatre was highly respected and well supported by the local community.

Every so often, the two of them would host a game night. Those members of the theatre group still left with time on their hands thoroughly enjoyed a round of Cluedo or charades. Mid-year, the entire company would become involved in a Murder in a Box dinner party, held in the theatre itself.

There were just five of them on this particular evening. Paul and Des had been invited to join in with Balderdash. Geoffrey also asked Rhonda along. She made her living by cleaning various venues, including William's two businesses in the mall. Rhonda was so kind and knew absolutely everybody. A member of the theatre company specialising in props, she adored Geoffrey and Martin and was always grateful for a social invitation.

"Everyone is looking forward to Lady Bracknell meets Lady Gaga," said Paul to Geoffrey. Paul was referring to their latest production. Geoffrey had suggested the idea of putting on a music hall–style event, where well-known characters from stage plays delivered a hit number. Paul and Des had decided on Romeo and Juliet singing Sonny and Cher's "I Got You, Babe." Rehearsals were proving the idea to be a winner.

"I reckon there won't be a theatre company in the country not copying the idea. Could we market it somehow?" Des suggested after two rounds of Balderdash.

"Spoken like a true treasurer!" Martin laughed. "I agree, though. It's brilliant. All ready for crackers and cheese? I'll get them, and then," Geoffrey added a little mysteriously, "I have a fresh idea for a little play I think you might enjoy becoming involved in."

CHAPTER 6

" They should all fit, I think." Robert and Alan were loading Sylvia and Vivienne's luggage into the car boot. Discovering the two friends needed to catch a late afternoon flight on Saturday, Robert had suggested that he take them to the airport. He had a pick up at around four o'clock. Robert reasoned that William needn't even know.

"I suppose it's all the hurried preparations and everything," Vivienne remarked, "but it hasn't hit me yet. When Tom picks us up, I might fall apart."

Sylvia liked Tom well enough. The five-year age difference when they were growing up meant that he was off playing with mates of similar age. Sylvia and Vivienne were happy to be left to their own devices.

"I wonder if we'll get to see Lola." Lola had lived close by, but as children, they hadn't seen much of each other outside of school.

"You mean Lovely Lola Lewis from Lexington Lane." Vivienne emphasised the alliteration as they had done as children, much to Lola's annoyance.

"Stop saying that!" Sylvia said, carrying on with the familiar childhood mimicry. "It's not Lexington Lane; it's Lexington Road." Lola would turn red with anger and run home in a huff. "We were a bit mean, to be honest." They both reminisced about some of the other characters they had left behind.

Alan and Robert were seated in the front of the car. "I couldn't agree more," Alan said to Robert. "Delvine is not at all what I was expecting." Seeing as the dealership was closed on Saturday afternoons, Alan felt he should accompany Sylvia to lend his support and make it less awkward for Robert, who didn't know either of the two women. "The suggestions she came up with for the staffroom were sensible. I got the impression she had every intention of dealing with customers."

Alan's head was full of turmoil. It didn't happen so often now. Most of the time, he could accept that Nina was gone from his life forever. He had to make the best of it. Alan didn't love Sylvia. He didn't think Sylvia loved him either. Still, it gave them a significant other in both of their lives. Settling was sometimes all there was.

The motorhome started it off this time. Alan could see Nina's face lighting up at the thought of a little weekend getaway. She wouldn't care how modern or luxurious it was (and in this case, it wasn't). She would merely relish the prospect of no one knowing where they were for a few days. Now Sylvia would be away for a couple of weeks. With no one else to fill the void, Nina would become his obsession once more. It scared him.

Ben threw the ball for Prince yet again. He had already spent an hour in the park. Even the dog struggled to gain his full attention. The new-car dealership was open all day Saturday, left in the capable hands of the assistant manager. Ben had relived his encounter with Delvine several times. The five minutes he had persuaded her to sit for had turned into thirty.

Delvine, Ben had discovered, was on the run. To be more precise, she was on the run from someone who was on the run. She had woken up one morning to the familiar sight of Johnny hastily shoving stuff into a holdall. He was urging her to get a bloody move on and do the same. She packed her bag without rushing, cleaning her teeth in the cracked basin of the seedy "guest house," which she was quite certain doubled as a brothel. Looking at her reflection in the mirror, she hardly recognised herself anymore.

"You got the money for the landlady, babe? See if you can knock her down a bit." The image of the "landlady," Tamzyn, came into Devine's mind. She imagined Tamzyn had once been quite lovely. Her hair would have been sleek and blonde, her skin flawless, her curvaceous figure the envy of many. Gradually her hair had become overbleached and listless, her skin sallow, and her body hidden beneath copious caftan-style garments.

Picking up her holdall, she surveyed her surroundings. Crap. Which just about summed up her life. She remained where she stood and contemplated Johnny for a while.

Johnny seemed to sense her scrutiny. "Babe, we've got to get a fuckin' move on. *Come on!* Shift it!"

"Goodbye, Johnny. Don't go trying to find me—although it's not as if you'd bother anyway, is it?" She hauled her meagre supply of luggage down the stairs. A dumbfounded Johnny stood on the landing staring after her.

"Babe ... Don't do this. Don't go. I love you."

Delvine unfastened the latch and walked out, leaving the door wide open.

"Can you lend me a fifty? Babe?"

That was almost a week ago. Begging a room from the only reliable friend she had left meant she at least had a roof over her head. She had to get work, but it was proving elusive. She had no qualifications to speak of, no references. If she didn't find something soon, she would have to go back to her parents, which, to be honest, was only marginally better than being with Johnny.

"As a matter of fact, I-I might know of a job," Ben found himself saying.

Delvine scoffed. "Sure you do. You own a bar and need waitresses. Supply your own skimpy uniforms. No, thanks." She stood and made to go. "Your dog wants to play." Prince was looking from one to the other of them expectantly.

"No, no, please. I'm serious. General office duties."

"That's a good name for it, I must say. Who's the general? You, I suppose?"

"No. Honestly." Ben always carried business cards. He handed her two. "This one is mine, and this one is my brother's. That's where the job is."

"You are kidding, right? In my experience, no such thing as a lucky coincidence."

Delvine was cleaning and sorting the pantry, while Rachel did the same with the fridge.

"I'm not going to be surprised if it all goes tits up. I mean, you know what a cynic I am, Rachel. First I'm sitting at the bus stop scrolling on my phone, no idea what to do. Your contact seems to scream at me. I wanted to see you so much; it's been so long. But hey, I can't just phone up when I need a place to stay and hope you'll be nice about it. So I phone you up and beg for a place to stay, and you're so nice about it!"

Rachel smiled. She liked Delvine and was glad she had called.

"I know I've got to find a decent job, cos there's no way I'm sponging off you. So there I am, probably looking far too desperate. No one gives me a chance. I end up at the park in tears, thinking I'll have to swallow my pride and go back home to Mum and put up with all the recriminations. Then I get hit by a ball thrown by a maniac exercising his dog. Naturally, he offers me a bloody job. Crazy!"

Rachel laughed and held on to her tummy. The baby wriggled. She wondered if the baby was laughing too.

"*And* you've got clothes I can borrow because they don't fit you anymore!"

"Dee, have you never thought that actions bring about circumstances? It does sound far-fetched, I know. But you wasted three years of your life with that jerk. Okay, he was charming and generous at the beginning. There were restaurants and perfume. But gradually he just became— sorry—a petty criminal, if the truth be told. You were always running away from someone he owed money to or avoiding the cops. He used you, Dee. Maybe taking control has brought about a whole new set of options. You chose to walk out and chose to ring me; you went out looking for a job and came home with one, admittedly from an unusual source. Stop thinking you don't deserve a chance and give it a fair go. Ooooh …" She arched her back and stretched out her muscles. "I'm hungry."

Alan had half an hour to kill before boarding the bus to the train station. Aimlessly wandering around duty-free stores seemed pointless after a few minutes. He may as well wait at the bus stop. Some of the smaller stores were closing up and screening off their premises. At the closest exit to the bus stop, there was a minimart stocked with essential items such as milk, teabags, and bread. Alan thought it was brilliant. How many people must disembark and have nothing in the house to see them through until morning? The rear of the store carried inexpensive pharmaceuticals and cosmetic brands for those refusing to pay exorbitant prices, duty-free or not. Another section of the store had stands of greeting cards and wrapping paper, a bargain box of bestsellers, and several brightly painted buckets stocked with flower arrangements.

A delicately boned woman wearing black leggings beneath a simple T-shirt dress was sorting through the bouquets. She removed some and put them into a separate bucket. Her back was towards Alan, but her short elfin haircut caught his eye because it reminded him of … "No," he whispered audibly. Alan closed his eyes, counted to five, and then forced himself to look again. "Think rationally. You know it isn't Nina. She's gone." And indeed, she was gone. No one was attending to any of the flower arrangements. He must get a grip on himself. Stability. Routine. He must keep busy. He would not fall in a hole again.

Alan walked to the bus stop and stood in the queue. He was glad of the slightly chilly wind. It seemed to aid his sense of logic. The bus arrived on time. A woman ahead of him in the queue struggled with several bags and a large case. He was glad to assist.

Settling into his seat, he remembered that one of his favourite TV dramas was beginning the third series at eight thirty. He could see into the minimart from where he sat. He watched as the same woman came through from the back of the store. She smiled at a customer who had selected a card and had begun looking at the floral displays. He was farther away now, of course. But there was something in the way she moved. Surely it couldn't be her. Alan felt his whole body react. There was no doubt. It was Nina.

CHAPTER 7

PERTH, WESTERN AUSTRALIA, SUNDAY

Delvine, Rachel, and Matthew breakfasted on cereal. Some women worked virtually until the first contraction. Although she loved her work as college chaplain at King James High School, she was glad to know that maternity leave would allow her time before and after the birth of their baby.

"I was on crowd control at a gig. A fight broke out between two guys. Bandit and I broke it up. They were young. Drunk. I took them to the wagon and told them if one parent would come for each of them and take them home, I wouldn't arrest them and keep them overnight in a police cell. Scared them witless. Rachel was nearby with St John's ambulance. She knew one of the guys and was a calming influence. Not so much love at first sight as love at first arrest!"

Delvine was so pleased to see how happy they were.

"You left the love of your life, I understand."

"More like I left a complete jerk. I can't believe it took me so long."

"Oh, we can all easily become embroiled. You know about the frog and the warm water gradually heating up?" Bandit sat dutifully at Matt's feet.

"Now, I mean this, guys. I'm sure you've discussed it without me. I can be gone in a couple of days if you've had a change of heart."

"It gives me peace of mind knowing that Rachel isn't alone so much. Shifts and overtime aren't fun, especially now with Fatso on the way!" Matthew quickly opened the door, dodged outside, and put some biscuits in a bowl for Bandit. Making a fuss of the working dog come family pet, Matthew smiled mischievously at Rachel. She hated his chosen nickname for their unborn baby. Bandit reciprocated by wagging his tail enthusiastically. A police officer with the canine unit, Matthew enjoyed the combination of skills the job offered.

"We're helping each other out. It has to be good, at least for now." Rachel began clearing the table.

"Leave that for me. You'll be late for church. You okay with my cobbling something together for lunch when you both get back?"

"How about you show your dad that YouTube footage of Sophie at her Gymkhana—and the photos on Facebook?" Suzanne suggested to Jade.

"Oh yeah, Dad. Come and look. Sophie looks so cool on her pony. She's called him Titbit. Stupid name. I'd call my pony Furlong. It's an old-fashioned word for something …"

"It's an archaic term of measurement, Jade. I'll watch it, but you're not getting a pony." The silent exchange of looks between mother and daughter did not go unnoticed by Ben. He knew they would keep wearing away at his resolve. But she was not getting a pony, and she was not joining the pony club. If he gave in, eventually there would be three girls riding horses around some bloody paddock somewhere.

Having been granted the shared rights of an empty cereal packet, Pearl and Opal headed for the craft corner, a refashioned built-in breakfast nook retained during the renovation. The intent was "to facilitate a collaboration of artistic abilities, resulting in the transformation of something ordinary into something beautiful." Suzanne had picked that up at a sibling unity workshop run by the Concerned Parent Group. Opal had managed to get access to the cardboard first. She was holding it high out of Pearl's reach while attempting to grab the pink scissors with the fancy cutting edge.

"It's half *mine!*" yelled Pearl. "Give it back. *Opal!* Mum, Dad, Opal's not being fair. And those scissors are *mine*."

"I'll give you half." Opal feigned patience and doggedly kept the cardboard out of her sister's reach.

"You'll make your half bigger. You always do. *Daaaad.*"

Ben muttered a few profanities under his breath. Suzanne seemed to be ignoring the potential fight and was heading for the bedroom. Walking to the pantry and selecting one of the alternate cereal packets, he removed the wax paper bag, complete with its contents, screwed it down firmly, and placed it back on the shelf. He handed the empty cardboard box to Pearl. It was greater in size than the one commandeered by Opal. She promptly snatched it from Pearl and gave her the original. Opal didn't notice the less favourable switch, so he let it go. He loved Opal, of course, but she was an absolute little bitch at times.

Suzanne had secluded herself in their generously proportioned walk-in wardrobe. One by one, she opened the drawers of her jewellery case. Ben had given her most of the jewellery. Some of the pieces—in fact all of them—might prove to be quite valuable, she reasoned.

Alan had endured a restless night. He knew it was Nina. He had always presumed that she had moved interstate. She had relatives in South Australia and New South Wales. She may have stayed here, though, or gone away and returned. Whatever. It didn't matter. He had found her. The awful thing was, she didn't want anyone to find her. He paced around the house. He couldn't talk to anyone about it. God, this was torture. His phone rang.

"Yes?" he answered curtly. He hadn't looked at the caller ID.

"Mr. Meadows, it's Robert. I know it's a Sunday, but I wondered if you were at a loose end."

Alan wanted to scream down the line. "I'm not ... I don't—"

"Sorry. My bad. I just thought that with Sylvia away, you might—"

"No, Robert. I'm the one who should apologise. I didn't sleep well. What did you want to say?"

"Well, you know about me and the cricket, right?"

"Of course." Alan expected an invitation to an amateur game. It might be better to be around people.

"I do a lot of stuff around the clubhouse. It … erm … badly needs painting."

Alan didn't respond immediately. "Is this your idea of sucking up to the boss, Robert?" he finally asked. "Cos I have to tell you that this isn't the way it usually pans out, you know?"

"Is that a yes?" asked Robert.

"You're a cheeky bloody upstart, Robert. I'm not buying the paint!" Alan laughed in spite of himself. "You pick me up and drop me off."

"You did me a favour today. Cheeky devil." Alan was helping Robert with cleaning up the brushes and rollers. It had been a good day's work.

"Well, with Sylvia away, you'd probably mope. No offence intended."

"None taken." Robert, of course, had no idea of the truth. Far from moping for Sylvia, Alan was yearning for Nina.

"Just a thought, boss. I reckon there's enough paint here in this tub to do the staffroom."

"Are you offering to do it, then?"

"Yeah. I reckon I owe you one."

Sylvia was not a frequent flier. She had packed, unpacked, and repacked several times. Her full suitcase was indicative of too much clothing. She was sure she would not wear half of what was in it. Having crammed a lot into an overnight bag to take on the flight, Vivienne had reminded her that they were inconveniently seated in the central block, with fellow passengers on either side. Most flight requirements had to be located in a small bag and stored under the seat in front. She was surprised to see several people carrying pillows on board.

Vivienne's business required her to travel often. Sylvia felt gauche by comparison. Both had looked through a magazine, watched a movie, eaten something unrecognisable, used the loo, and slept. Indeed, after attempting sleep, Sylvia appreciated the notion of bringing a personal pillow.

"So, apart from making the obvious arrangements, have you managed to speak a fair bit to your mum?" Vivienne was offering Sylvia a butterscotch lozenge.

Sylvia took her time unwrapping the welcome treat. "Yum. Thanks. You've thought of everything. Mind you, you didn't bring a pillow!"

"No. This small inflatable one suits me." Viv screwed up the wrapper and tucked it into the webbed receptacle on the rear of the seat facing her. "So have you ... talked?"

"Well, it's all happened quickly, hasn't it? I mean, I haven't had much of a chance. I'm going to ring for water. Want one?"

LONDON UK

"I hope you don't mind English Breakfast. I can easily get something else tomorrow if you have a particular favourite." Rebecca selected two of the four non-matching but classically styled cups and saucers from the wide ledge beneath the kitchen window. She placed them on the table where Sylvia sat.

"English Breakfast is fine. Thanks, Mum." Sylvia took in the room. It was familiar, yes, yet very different from what she had remembered. "It looks lovely in here."

"Well, I've no one to please but myself, Sylvia." The fragments of furniture familiar to Sylvia had been painted white. Two relatively inexpensive white wicker sofas, of the kind usually reserved for patios, looked comfortable and inviting. Shades of blue in cushions and wall hangings created a sense of calm.

"I've arranged for a few days off to give us a bit of time. We need it, I think." Rebecca poured the tea from a pot.

"Yes. The shock's been awful." Sylvia watched her mother add milk to her own and then pass it to her. "But what do you mean? Why do you have to ask for time off? You work from home."

"I haven't worked from home for two years, Sylvia. Oh, sorry. Would you like a biscuit?"

Sylvia was stunned. "No. No, thanks. So where do you work, then?"

"Homespun. It's one of those superstores. Everything related to sewing, craft, you know. A short walk to the station, two stops, a short walk at the other end." Rebecca took a few sips of tea. Seeing as Sylvia appeared lost for words, she continued. "They advertised for sales staff when they first opened. I decided to give it a go. After I'd been there for a year, they offered me a promotion. I run the home furnishing section. Nine till five, Monday through Friday." She took a few more sips of tea.

Sylvia recovered herself. "God, Mum. Why didn't you say anything? How come I didn't know?"

"I suppose because … you never asked."

CHAPTER 8

"I'll stay behind tonight and paint the walls. It shouldn't take too long," Robert explained to Delvine as she was tidying up the customer coffee corner.

"I'd be happy to help. If you'd like, that is. I've got a bit of a project mentality."

"Oh. It would be great to have someone to talk to." Robert immediately felt embarrassed. He had sounded patronising.

"And would you let me hold the ladder steady as well?" Delvine laughed.

"Sorry. That came out wrong. I've got some overalls, but you've only got your good clothes with you. Did you check out the brochure, by the way?"

"Yes. I wrote down a few things, but it's not my money."

"Let's see if we can strike while the iron is hot, shall we?" Robert looked out the window at Alan discussing stock with Neville. Alan had seemed very upbeat this morning, as if given a chance to sell a Bond car or something, which was odd, considering that Sylvia was away.

"That's three for the car lot, then, and two for scrap," Neville confirmed. "Now, about the camper van ... I don't think it will sell from here. It needs to go to a caravan dealership. I'll take it—"

"No. Please. Don't take it anywhere." Alan was surprised at his depth of feeling concerning an unremarkable motorhome. He was aware of Neville's confusion. "I have had an enquiry, as a matter of fact." Although this was untrue, he had to say something to justify keeping it.

"You serious?" Neville laughed.

"Yes. An elderly couple. I said I'd keep it for a week."

Alan was in turmoil. He was sure he had seen Nina. Maybe he should let sleeping dogs lie. He wanted her to see him. Could that be enough? If at least she knew he'd seen her, then what? There was some inexplicable link between Nina and the motorhome. If he let the motorhome go, she would go too. He knew it was illogical. He sounded crazy, even to himself. He would drive up to the airport tonight. He had to.

There was no denying that business was good at Meadows Motors. The new-car dealership and corporate section was well located and enjoyed a well-earned reputation for reliability and customer service. The used-car aspect of the business offered good deals and had plenty of vehicles on its books at a time. Customers were rarely disappointed. Neville's mob was great with repairs, maintenance, and roadside assistance, as well as efficiently taking care of scrap, which also turned in a profit. An office in the main building dealt with warranties, insurance, and just about anything else related to owning a car. Ben worked hard overseeing the whole and justified his "dalliances" as harmless bits of fun. Until now.

"I just felt I should check with you before spending the money on a staffroom upgrade. But to be honest, it's well overdue. The staff needs space to store personal belongings, especially female staff," Alan added pointedly. He had taken the trouble to walk across to Ben's office rather than speak to him on the phone. It seemed obvious that Delvine was different from all the others he had been asked to accommodate. He owed it to her and to himself to treat her like a valued staff member, and Ben could bloody well lump it. "Delvine also suggested that we purchase a few things to create a kiddie corner. Apparently, she knows where to get some stuff second-hand."

"Delvine is … erm … settling in well, then?"

"Absolutely." Alan was aware that it was early days, but he so rarely experienced the upper hand as far as Ben was concerned.

"Sounds good to me. When it's completed, call me. I'll see for myself."

Walking back to the lot, Alan felt almost euphoric. It was just as well that Ben had approved the upgrade, for Alan had already given the go-ahead to Robert and Delvine. Experiencing one of those episodes where he felt himself to be the master of his destiny, Alan could make things happen. Beneath all his positive self-affirmation, of course, was Nina—and the thought that she would come back into his life if he played his cards right.

Alan arranged for one of the mechanics to take Delvine to the office supply company to pick up their goods. Delvine found some plastic overalls and disposable gloves. Alan paid for pizza delivery and told Delvine she could take the following morning off in lieu.

Suzanne felt altogether more in control by lunchtime. Driving to a jewellery store on the other side of town after the school run was sensible. It was unlikely that she might see any familiar faces. Not that she was doing anything untoward, of course. She no longer wanted to wear the jewellery pieces in her bag. Once the weight of the gold was known, she would receive their full value in cash. The cash would go directly into the bank, and the Christmas fund would be set to rights once more. Suzanne resolved that she would forgo her clothing allowance and redistribute it to the girls for the rest of the year, thereby making up for any shortfall. (Well, almost.)

Returning home, Suzanne attacked the family laundry with close to religious fervour. There had been a slight problem. She had sorted it. It would never happen again, she told herself.

PERTH, WEST AUSTRALIA, TUESDAY

"You're an early bird!" chirped Robert to Alan as he walked into the office.

"I was anxious to view your handiwork." Alan was standing in the doorway of the freshly painted staffroom. A coat of white paint had transformed all four beige walls. The room appeared more spacious. A steel grey unit comprised of four lockers with storage space beneath had been placed against one wall. Next to it leant a plain mirror with adhesive backing, waiting to be put in place when the paint was thoroughly dry. Three small stools underneath a shallow bench table adjusted to bar height sat against the opposite wall. A neat square coffee table stood on a variegated grey rectangular rug, creating a centrepiece. On either side of the table was a comfortable small chair in charcoal grey.

"Well done. Consider your debt to be paid in full!" Alan nodded towards the kiddie-friendly corner. A roadway play mat and three brightly coloured boxes took up about two square metres. The boxes contained small cars, a set of connecting blocks, and some books. "That looks good too," he commented. "Courtesy of the Salvation Army, by any chance?"

"Save the Children, I think," Robert said. "Charity shop anyway. The grey rug came from there as well. I'd better get on with the chores if Delvine is having half a day off—well deserved, I reckon." Robert shuffled his feet a little awkwardly and went off to attend to the cleaning duties.

It was true that Alan wanted to see the minor refurbishments. However, the real reason for his early start was insomnia. His foray to the airport had proved a fruitless exercise. He had spent three hours drinking coffee and feigning interest in magazines. Whenever he finished a coffee, he would wander around close to the corner store where he had seen Nina. The flowers were there, but she wasn't. A security officer began eyeing him up. There could be all sorts of reasons for her not being there. Part of him felt that he should leave well alone. But he knew he couldn't. Even if she saw him, told him to go away, and never attempt to see her again, he had to try.

By mid-morning, two sales had been completed. Alan was going through a file of papers that Robert had found when he was decorating. He didn't want to throw them out without checking with Alan first. The door buzzer sounded. Alan looked up to see Ben looking around the office floor critically.

"Oh, hi, Ben. This is an unexpected pleasure. I was going to invite you to view the new staffroom this afternoon. Can I get you a coffee?" Alan deliberately tidied up the papers he had been sifting through and gave Ben his full attention.

"No, no, thanks I'm fine. The car lot looks good. Excellent, in fact."

"Do you want to see the staffroom, then?" Alan crossed the floor and opened the door. Robert was cleaning down the mirror after adhering it to the wall.

"Good morning, Mr. Meadows. Can I get you a coffee? You might want to try out one of our new chairs." Robert made a show of presenting the chairs as if they were a prize on an old-style game show. "Come on down!"

"No coffee, thank you, Robert. Good job. Thank you. For the time, I mean."

Robert did not know Ben well, but glancing at Alan, he could sense the awkwardness between them. Alan was confident enough. After all, this was his domain. But he was not sure how to handle Ben.

"The kiddie corner is new too. Delvine took charge of that." Alan immediately regretted mentioning her name.

"She was a big help with the staffroom as well," Robert added, shutting the staffroom door and looking at Alan sheepishly. He was grateful to see someone drive onto the grounds. "Duty calls." Robert breathed a sigh of relief and made a hasty exit.

"Is Delvine not here?" Ben was looking out over the cars as if expecting her to poke her head out from underneath one of them.

"Oh, no. I gave her the morning off." Alan wasn't going to offer any apology or protracted explanation.

"Sweet." Ben kept up his overview of the cars. "I'd just like to thank her, you know, in person."

CHAPTER 9

"I'm just saying I'm a little surprised, that's all." Vivienne was washing up. Tom was drying and stacking.

"Bed and breakfasts aren't a walk in the park, Viv. Mum's always saying how exhausting it is. More often than not, they do the evening meal as well. People like it. Three courses usually, plus coffee. They have up to six or more people at a time. It's on the go from early till late."

"You don't have to convince me that they work hard, Tom. I know that. They've always worked hard. But Joe and Bibi are their parents, for God's sake, not distant relations. They won't be here until a few hours before the funeral tomorrow, and then they're leaving a few hours afterwards. It seems disrespectful."

"Well, they knew we'd be here."

"Yes. But you've taken time off work. I've flown halfway around the world. Apart from the service itself, all the arrangements have been left to us. There's been a lot to do. Surely they would have contingency plans for any emergencies? After all, we're the grandchildren. We're grieving too, aren't we?"

"Keep your voice down. Bibi will hear." Bibi was resting on the sofa in the front room.

"And that's another thing." Viv lowered her voice to a dramatic stage whisper. "Where's the consideration for Bibi? Have they even

49

mentioned the fact that she has an injury? And what will she do now that she hasn't got Joe?"

"I don't know. I expect Mum and Dad have thought about it. We'll have to talk as a family tomorrow, I suppose."

Tomorrow, Vivienne pondered. *In the car on the way to the crematorium? Or on the return journey?*

"I'm checking times with the caterers," Tom said. "I'll use the landline."

Bibi twisted her body around to try to get more comfortable. She wished she could sleep, but it evaded her. Weddings and funerals, she supposed, brought out the best and the worst in people. Along with Joe, she had felt thrilled with the union of their son, Peter, with Meg. She recalled the occasion when Peter had brought Meg home to meet them. He was besotted. They had met as London tour guides for the summer season. Both of them held ambitions for owning a travel company.

It was not until both Vivienne and Tom were born that Bibi had realised how utterly used she had been. It wasn't manipulation by Meg and capitulation on behalf of Joe and Bibi. Instead, it was pure presumption. The house was generously proportioned. Over the years, it had been added to, divided, and adapted to suit the family needs. Bibi couldn't recall her permission or preference ever being sought on one single occasion.

"Oh, you're awake, Bibi. I'll bring you a cup of tea." The sprain had not been quite as bad as was first thought, but her badly bruised ankle was painful. "You don't look comfortable. Would one of the chairs be better?" Viv plumped up the cushions and made to put her arms around Bibi.

"No, thank you. I'm all right. I'd rather sit in the other room with you."

"Oh, of course. I just thought you would want it quiet."

"Vivvy, I've got no idea what to wear tomorrow. You know, for the funeral."

"Oh my goodness, Bibi. What kind of a granddaughter am I? I'm hopeless, that's what! Okay, let's move into the other room. I'll make your tea, and you can suggest a couple of outfits. I'll get them down from upstairs, and we'll 'workshop some ideas.'" They both laughed. Bibi considered how unlike her mother Vivienne was.

Repairing to the large area at the back of the house, which served as kitchen/dining as well as the main living and TV room, they discovered that Tom was in the process of making tea. He had half listened into their conversation.

"I can make tea," he said, locating a tin of biscuits from the pantry, "but if it's all the same to you, I'll forgo the wardrobe melee! I've confirmed the caterers, by the way."

"Thank you, Tom." Bibi felt she had earned the right to be proud of them both, seeing as she was the one who had raised them.

Peter and Meg started their travel business just after their children were born, having learned the ropes with established companies. They came up with ten-day budget holidays to France and Italy, with a twist. Promoted as Tutelage Breaks, they focused on various academic pursuits. Crash courses in fine arts, art history, ancient Rome, and the Renaissance were a huge hit. It was not often with cash-poor students; far more frequently, it was with middle-income earners who felt enriched by the European experience. They were brilliant at it. Having made good money, they decided a few years ago to change their lifestyle and opt for running a bed and breakfast establishment. To their dismay, they found it every bit as stressful and not nearly as lucrative.

"Should we call in next door to see if we can help this afternoon?" Sylvia asked Jessica. They were compiling a shopping list for the next few days.

"There are plenty of them there, Sylvia. Too many cooks and all that … I've only instant coffee, I'm afraid. I can't be bothered with all that coffee machine paraphernalia, and I don't exactly have heaps of spare work surface space."

"Oh, I'm quite happy with tea. I find it more refreshing." Sylvia drew a leafy pattern on the shopping list notepad. "Mum, is everything all right with you and Bibi?"

"Bibi? Of course. Are you still more into cheese and biscuits than chocolate? You'd better add crackers to the list."

"It's just that, well, you've hardly mentioned them."

"Isn't it annoying when you find two unopened packets of something and only half a packet of something else you know you'll need?" Rebecca shifted a few things around on the middle shelf of the pantry.

"Am I putting my foot in it here? Is there something I should know about?" Sylvia watched her mother cross to the sink. She rinsed a sponge under the hot tap, then returned to the cupboard and began wiping out the shelf.

"Mum?"

Rebecca stopped cleaning and looked directly at Sylvia. "Why don't you fill me in on Alan? I want to hear everything about him."

"Mum. Sit down, please, and tell me exactly what's up."

"Bibi." Meg hugged her mother-in-law a little awkwardly, as she wasn't able to stand. Bibi winced with the discomfort. "So sorry. So sorry." Releasing Bibi from her embrace momentarily, Meg looked her in the eye and shook her head as if no words of comfort were to be found. She then embraced her once more. Bibi winced again.

Bibi wondered if the painkillers she had taken were ill advised, as she felt her stomach turn quite violently. Peter stood back a little until Meg drew away from Bibi and asked Viv if the kettle was on. Kneeling in front of her, Peter took Bibi's hands in his. They had spoken a few times on the phone since the accident. The tears welled up in Bibi's eyes, and she began to sob. Peter hugged her. "I'm sorry we weren't here for you, Mum."

Meg watched Vivienne make the tea. "Thank you for stepping in as soon as you could, Vivvy. Sorry we couldn't get away sooner."

"They were outstanding in the hospital. I'm not sure they would keep someone in for observation that long under normal circumstances. Once Tom was here, of course, he could take charge."

"Of course. Yes. Of course. Tom is very reliable. We couldn't leave everything, you see. We had two families right up until this morning. We left at dawn. They were accommodating. They even agreed to have a continental breakfast. Mind you, our continental is a cut above the average. Mrs. Hobbs attended to all the last minute details. She's a godsend. Salt of the earth."

Vivienne set the tea on the table. "It must have been a terrible shock for you both."

"Well, yes. More for Peter, of course. I mean ..." Meg moved a cup and saucer closer to her as she sat at the table. It struck Vivienne that her mother had offered no words of sympathy towards either herself or Tom.

"We shall have to return tomorrow. It would look a bit odd to rush off straight away. Is a bed made up?"

"Yes. I made one up just in case."

"I might go and lie down for a bit after my tea."

The back door rattled open. A flushed but rather jubilant Tom manoeuvred his way into the kitchen carrying a folding wheelchair.

"One chariot for one invalid. Hello, Mum. You made it in good time, then."

CHAPTER 10

PERTH, WESTERN AUSTRALIA, WEDNESDAY

Nina was admiring the bold colours of the gerberas she was arranging, along with Geraldton wax for greenery and baby's breath for filler. She loved the bright wrapping paper too. Flowers were the best gift ever, she always thought. How could flowers not impress anyone?

"Here's the list for the hotel, Nina. Big one. The usual three for the foyer, plus the wedding booking. A couple of rooms have booked arrangements. There's a complimentary for an upgrade and the usual half dozen small bouquets for the hotel gift shop. Busy, busy! I'm going to increase the hospital kiosk delivery. An extra, say, four each time." Deb managed Bouquets, suppliers of excellent quality floral decorations and so on for several outlets and two hotels. The business operated from a shop in town with a small upstairs flat shared by Deb and Nina.

"Great. I was wondering if we should increase the airport delivery. I think there's a real market for potentially apologetic husbands." Nina smiled. "Seriously!"

"Go for it, then," suggested Deb. "An extra two each time, maybe."

Talk of the airport brought Nina's mind back to a few days ago, when she had experienced the odd feeling of being watched. She didn't feel threatened at all, strangely enough. There were security guards around, not to mention plenty of people. She hadn't seen any suspicious behaviour, merely sensed a sort of presence.

Deb and Nina were flat out keeping the business going. There was little time for rest and recreation. Having walked away from an abusive relationship, Deb vowed and declared that she would remain self-sufficient and single for the rest of her days.

After leaving Alan, Nina had retreated home to her parents in New South Wales. A year ago, she had decided to return. She had been unfair to Alan, she knew, but could see no way to put things right. At the time, everything was so awful that it didn't make sense to come back to the "scene of the crime," as it were. She couldn't find forgiveness, but maybe she could at least try to explain. Once here, however, her resolve faltered. She didn't deserve a second chance.

"Can we move those three blue motors to the front of the yard, please, Robert? They're in great nick and will look fantastic in a group."

"Too easy, boss. I'll use the wheel ramps, shall I?"

Ben interrupted them. He sauntered in almost as if he wanted to buy a vehicle himself.

"Ben!" Alan wasn't quite sure how to greet him. His presence was unusual at the best of times. Twice in as many days seemed distinctly odd. "We were discussing the promotion of three excellent cars we've got on the books."

At that moment, Delvine rushed in, appearing quite flustered. "I am so sorry, Mr. Meadows. Oh, good morning, Mr. Meadows!" Delvine straightened her jacket and held out her hand to Ben. It's good to see you and say a proper thank you for placing your trust in me. I apologise, everyone, for being a little late. Two people arguing about the ownership of a travel ticket held up the bus. I thought it would be quicker to get off and walk the last bit. Sorry." Delvine made to move towards the staffroom.

"No worries," said Alan. He was about to make a joke about the intrinsic value of a travel ticket when Ben interjected.

"Are you telling me that you don't own a car, Ms. Delvine?"

Delvine laughed. "No, Mr. Meadows. I don't own a car. I'm afraid it's out of the question at the moment.

Alan and Robert exchanged confused looks. Not only was Ben an unexpected caller; he and Delvine did not appear to share any intimacy. He wasn't aware that she had no vehicle. She didn't expect him to know anything about her particular circumstances. It was all quite peculiar.

"We can do something about that, can't we Alan? We're surrounded by cars, after all!" Ben chuckled. That was peculiar too. Ben didn't often make amusing comments. "There must be a little bargain out there somewhere with Devine's name on it, right? Robert, take a tour of the yard with Delvine and select a suitable vehicle, would you? I'll discuss the finances with Mr. Meadows."

Once Robert and Delvine were out of earshot, Alan looked Ben squarely in the face. "Talk to me. And don't give me any bullshit."

Delvine allowed herself to be shunted out through the main door by a perplexed Robert and away into the central section of the yard before she had a chance to get her thoughts together. They both looked at each other awkwardly for a moment. Robert was pleased there were no potential customers around.

"This is ridiculous, Robert." Delvine's eyes were fiery. "There is no way, *no way*, I'm accepting a car. I mean, what's he thinking? I'm grateful for the job and everything, but I'm not … Hang on. Is that it? Does he think I'll …?"

"What? Does he think you'll what?"

"Robert. You're not stupid. Does he think I'll, you know, show my gratitude?" She spat out the last few words.

"Oh. God. No. I'm sure. I mean, we didn't know …"

"Who's *we*? And know what?"

"Well, how you—"

A car pulled into the yard and chortled to a stop. Robert presumed that the two adults in the front of the car were parents to the three little ones in the back. "Look, I must deal with this. If you can't go back into the office, can you look busy? Sorry." He took a notepad and pen from his pocket, handed it to her, and made his way over to the newly arrived family. Delvine reluctantly began jotting down useless information about some of the vehicles. She could see Ben and Alan through the main door. Ben appeared to be doing all the talking.

"Anyway, that's how we met. I just felt so sorry. Offering the girl a job seemed like the right thing to do." Ben glanced out into the yard. "In the circumstances."

"The circumstances being that you fancied her." Alan kept looking straight at him. "She's a nice girl, Ben."

"I know, I know."

"And she's young."

"I know."

"And you're *married*!" Alan let the remark hang in the air. "I think that right now you should leave by the back door, and I'll come and see you at the end of the day. Maybe we can work something out. About a vehicle, I mean. I was beginning to think Delvine could be a real asset. But none of us need the complication of you fooling around with her." Alan surprised himself. He was not going to let Ben off lightly.

Once Ben had left the premises, Alan went out into the yard to smooth things over with Delvine and Robert. He found Robert and the male customer talking animatedly about the car in which they had arrived. Delvine was with the mother and children, who were excitedly trying out the seating arrangements in an eight-seater people mover. He moved back inside and left them to it.

"There's the school run, of course. But it doesn't stop there. Jason started footy, so all of them will expect to do extra things soon. We need a sound, roomy vehicle." The children's mother was watching the two eldest siblings quite carefully as they enthusiastically and repeatedly swapped places.

"And quite a robust one!" Delvine added with a smile as she held the little girls' hands and allowed her to climb onto the step and jump down.

Robert and the children's father walked towards them, both looking as pleased as punch. "So what do you think, babe? Shall we go for broke?"

"You mean even *more* broke!" They laughed together, and he picked up the little girl. "Well, there must be paperwork to do."

"The children can come inside while you deal with all of that." Delvine held out a hand to one of the boys, indicating it was time to move. She looked quite pointedly at Robert. "We have a small play area. They'll be fine. And you might both enjoy a coffee."

"Well, that didn't take nearly as long as I expected," the mother remarked to Delvine as they walked into the salesroom with the children in tow.

Delvine noticed that Alan had returned to his desk. The children spotted the play corner and made a beeline for the toys. "Please take a seat and I'll start on that coffee. Both with milk? Sugar?"

Ben made his way back to his office in a state of utter confusion. Realising he must have looked foolish to Alan, absurd to Robert, and, most importantly, a complete dickhead to Delvine, he was secretly appalled at himself. Recalling some of the brash, flirtatious, overtly willing females he had spent time with, he knew Alan was right. He was married with three girls. He might not be happily married, and his girls might disappoint him, but …

He could well imagine his inlaws' reaction should he attempt any form of separation. Frank, Suzanne's father, had put money into the business and continued to send significant patronage his way. Frank knew people. Good and bad. Ben had ingratiated his way into the family well enough, but if we were to get on his father-in-law's less charitable side, there would be serious repercussions. Gina, Suzanne's mother, would give him absolute hell and probably make sure the girls ended up hating him.

What was it with Delvine? She was lovely. Unpretentious. In truth, he couldn't analyse it. When he saw her, he felt like a different man. A better man. She was too young for him; he knew that. And she probably wouldn't go anywhere near a married man.

Upon reaching the showroom, he walked straight through to his office, closed the door, and poured himself a stiff drink, despite the hour. Picking up the phone, he requested that Alan be pencilled in for an appointment at 5:15 p.m. and asked for confirmation to be made with Alan.

Returning bottle and glass to their usual places, he straightened his jacket and tie and embarked upon a complete tour of every department. It kept his staff on their toes and helped him regain his sense of control—for now at least.

"There's one here that's gluten-free. But they are all labelled with a list of ingredients if you want to check for your peace of mind." Suzanne was assisting at the cake stall. Ten minutes to go until the end of the school day and almost everything was sold.

"Goodness, you've done well," commented Mrs. Bender. She was walking her class back from the library. "Line up at the door, please, everybody. Quietly, please." Suzanne was always amazed at how most teachers seemed to manage more than twenty children day in and day out without having a nervous breakdown. Mrs. Bender sidled up to Suzanne while keeping an eye on her class. "You can reduce the cost of the last few—we may as well get rid of them. Erm, Tony, I did say quietly, please." She re-joined her class as they lined up at the door.

Suzanne had been so pleased with her efforts at self-control. She knew she could do it. The computer had not been in use for days. Fair enough, she had bought a couple of scratch and win tickets at the news agency. In fact, she won five dollars. She probably should have kept the winnings, but it was only five dollars. Mrs. Robson, the doctor's wife, approached the stall.

"Not very much left? Well done. I'll take the rest. Let's see ..." Nora Robson calculated the amount in her head. "Twenty-eight dollars, I think." She pulled out her purse.

"Twenty-five will do, I'm sure," Suzanne suggested.

Mrs. Robson took a twenty and a ten from her purse and placed the money in Suzanne's hand. "Take thirty," she said. "It's for a good cause." The money raised was going towards the school's sponsored child.

Suzanne thanked her and wished her an enjoyable evening. She placed both the twenty and ten-dollar bills in the money tin, tidied the banknotes, and placed them in order of value. Parents seemed to be in a hurry or engaged in conversation. Her table was empty, so no one approached the stall. Looking around furtively, she removed the ten and twenty from the tin and tucked them into the pocket of her jeans. She was unaware of Mrs. Bender observing the whole scene from her classroom window.

CHAPTER 11

Alan had a distinct feeling that the tables had turned. On this occasion, he stood with his back towards the window of the new-car yard. Ben remained seated at his desk.

"It's been hard work talking Delvine down from the high ground, Ben. Whatever were you thinking?"

"She'll stay, though, won't she? It's a good deal." Ben was digitally signing off on an agreement he had drawn up.

Alan sighed audibly. "She's all right with it for now, Ben. But there must be no hint of any impropriety or expectation on your part. You do fully understand that, don't you?"

"Absolutely. Fully understood." A small black car in excellent condition was to be a working show vehicle. Embellished with the company name, number, and Web address, it was on loan to Delvine for as long as she remained in the company's employ. It was to be well kept, naturally.

Rachel shuffled the sales brochures and generic household notifications awkwardly as she watched Delvine draw up to the house and park the car. "What did you do to deserve that?" she asked Delvine, who slid out of the car and shut the door decisively.

"It's not what it looks like." Delvine used the remote to lock up. She couldn't hide the grin as she slung her bag over her shoulder.

"Actually, I hope it is what it looks like, Dee. A company car on loan—and nothing else."

"I wish you could have been there, Rachel. Mr. Meadows, the one from the park, was looking at the staffroom makeover. I was a bit late because … Well, anyway, he said I should have a car and could Mr. Meadows—my boss, his brother—find me one. I went completely mental—well, to Robert, not them—for the same reason as you're thinking, right? So … a bit later, Mr. Meadows, my boss, said he was sorry about the way it probably came across and I shouldn't feel in any way compromised."

Delvine looked away and moved towards the front door. "Shit." She let Rachel go ahead of her into the house. "Now I've said it to you, it does sound dicey. If it sounds too good to be true, it probably is. Shit."

"Well, maybe I've just got a suspicious mind. We can talk to Matt and get a male perspective. He'll be home soon."

Matthew walked in a few minutes later. "It needn't be dicey. Lots of firms do that kind of stuff." He had listened to the girls' story while he prepared food for the dog. "Admittedly, you've only been there five minutes, but …" He made a fuss of Bandit, who had waited patiently for permission to eat. "I'd play it cool if I were you and presume there is nothing suspect. It sounds like your immediate boss isn't going to cause you any problems anyway. Give them a fair go, eh?"

LONDON, UK WEDNESDAY

"Mum, I'm struggling to take all this in. How could I have been so ignorant about how hard it was for you? About how alone you must have felt?"

Rebecca was ironing the dress she planned to wear for the funeral. Sylvia was sitting on the bed, utilising the hair straightener she had added to her case.

"I should have had more to say about it at the time." Rebecca smoothed out the creases of one of her favourite cotton dresses. "Joe was long-distance lorry driving. Bibi missed him on his nights away. More often than not, Peter and Meg took turns in touring, but on their homestay weeks, they seemed to work on their tour preparations. At least that was what Bibi always said. In any case, it was Bibi who kept everything running smoothly."

"It's not occurred to me before, but she was virtually running a hotel for the six of them then, with very little help." Sylvia began running the tongs through her hair for a second time.

"Exactly. Washing, ironing, cleaning, cooking, and everything required for family life was down to her. Having you around to occupy Viv was a godsend for her. Tom was off with his mates, being that bit older. And you liked the busyness of it all, I think. Anyway, that was when you seemed happy. I could have insisted that you spent more time with me, but you probably would have resented it. Understandably."

"And you were here, left on your own, apart from the odd occasions when Dad would turn up?"

"Yes. Alone and bored." Rebecca hung her dress on a hanger to cool and picked up Sylvia's garment.

"Oh, Mum. That's so awful. And it stayed that way too, even when we left school? When I wasn't working, I was next door or out with Viv."

"I learnt to get used to it. Thought of it as my lot, I suppose. Your moving to Australia with Vivienne was merely the next step away from me. But applying for my job changed everything. I'm a different person, Sylvia. I have friends. I go boot-scooting every week and often go to a dance on Saturdays." Rebecca poured more water into the steam iron. "This material is lovely," she said, running her hands over the skirt before she began ironing it. "Now … I want to hear about Alan."

Sylvia rummaged in her case for her hairbrush. "There's not much to tell. He's an extremely likeable man, you know. Thoroughly decent and all that. Never really got over his first wife, though. She just left. Sometimes he gets all sort of ... I don't know. Maudlin, I suppose you'd say. Then other times he gets excited, as if she might walk in the door any moment. But he can be kind and caring too. If I walk out on him as well ..." Sylvia stood to run her fingers through the underside of her hair. She brushed and smoothed it, running her fingers through it again, this time from the top side.

"Your hair looks lovely, Sylvia."

"If you've got a drier, I can blow wave yours for you, if you like."

"I had to be quite persuasive in arranging the late service at the crematorium, Mum. They charged extra, of course." Tom was adjusting his tie in the mirror. The doorbell rang. "There are the cars now."

"Well, yes, people do, don't they? What does seem odd, though, is your grandfather prearranging everything for the service and insisting that no one else interfere in any way. Not even Bibi."

"He's become very friendly with the vicar of St Jude's over the last few years. Some men's group, I think. From what I can make out, the two of them put their heads together a few months ago and decided how they wanted their funerals to go, and no one else got a look in."

"Well, as long as there's nothing unseemly going on."

Tom couldn't help but wonder what his mother meant by "unseemly." Joe probably just had a few favourite hymns or a special poem lined up. He privately considered what was to happen with the eulogy, but he said nothing.

The journey to the crematorium took about twenty minutes. Two cars transported the family members, including Joe's elderly siblings and their wives. In both cars, the occupants discussed the weather, along with the occasional childhood memory. Being ushered to their places on arrival, however, they were surprised to see a relatively large gathering of people prepared to pay their respects.

Tom had thoughtfully asked that two chairs be removed to make space for Bibi's wheelchair. Once settled, a sense of quiet pervaded the chapel. The vicar of St Jude's took his place before the mourners and took his time looking about him. With each passing second, the vicar appeared to gain a sense of self-importance. He smiled.

"Joseph Blackwood, known to all of you here as Joe, was a man who prided himself on doing the right thing. We got to know each other well over the past few years. Often our conversations would turn to the inevitability of our eventual demise. Joe had very definite ideas about what he wanted to happen when it came to it, and he left clear instructions with me. Admittedly, Joe's sudden passing has been a shock to us all. Nonetheless, we shall fulfil his wishes. Joe has taken an unusual and, if I may say, a rather bold step by giving his eulogy personally. I invite you to listen respectfully."

He nodded towards the back of the chapel. Immediately a screen lit up in front of them all, with a photograph of Joe on it. Joe was indeed addressing the congregation in person. Several pictures from his past made up a fitting slideshow.

"You are here today to say goodbye to me. Thank you for coming," Joe began. "I've had a good life, and I'm grateful for it. But what it boils down to is this: I'm an ordinary man who worked hard and loved his family like thousands of others. I haven't made any groundbreaking discoveries or won any medals for courage. I haven't sacrificed my life for others. I have just soldiered on day by day and tried to do the right thing. It wasn't always easy.

"I don't want heaps of sad people saying farewell to me. You've shared in my life, and I've shared in yours. When it's my time to go, I want people to think of the good things and the good times." A smiling Joe giving a thumbs up sign caused a ripple of amused laughter. "I hope that when you do think of me after I've gone, it will be with genuine warmth. Even—ladies and gentlemen—when I've left the building."

The screen then became still, with one recent photograph of Joe remaining. Within seconds, orchestrated music began, filling the auditorium with the unmistakable sounds of Memphis. From a door to one side of the stage housing the rostrum, the floral displays, and the resplendently mounted coffin entered none other than Elvis Presley.

His familiar white suit glistened, and the rhinestones on his shoes twinkled. He held one hand aloft. A microphone in his remaining hand allowed for a bright and confident "Thank you very much, ladies and gentlemen. Thank you very much." Executing the famed swagger, hip swivel, and rotary arm movement with absolute perfection, Elvis began clicking his fingers and strutting his stuff about the stage as he broke into "Burning Love."

> *Lord Almighty, I feel my temperature rising.*
> *Higher, higher. It's burning through to my soul.*

Accompanied by backing music and singers courtesy of the technological expertise of sound technician Brian, he sounded convincing. The congregation was stunned, but not for long. They tapped their feet and swayed. Some clicked their fingers, a few joined in with the vocals, and two couples at the back stood up and danced.

The song finished, and then gradually the music became more solemn as Elvis ceased gyrating and deliberately took in the whole congregation, holding them enthralled.

> *Mine eyes have seen the glory of the coming of the Lord …*

It was the opening line of "The Battle Hymn of the Republic." Lyrics overlaid Joe's image. People began to stand. Soon everyone was on their feet and singing at the tops of their voices. There wasn't a dry eye in the house, with the exception of Bibi and her family. They remained seated in an utter state of confusion and shock. As the song reached its dramatic climax, the curtains drew to one side as Joe's coffin slowly moved away on its final journey.

> *Glory, glory, hallelujah …*

As they sang, they were so taken up with the emotional momentum of the truth marching on that they failed to notice the curtains closing. They clapped, whooped, and cheered until the music ended and there was silence once more.

The vicar of St Jude's, appearing a little red-faced, took the stage once more.

"Ahem. The family invites you to stay for refreshments, provided in the condolence lounge." He stepped down from the stage; shook hands with Bibi, Peter, and Meg; and made a hasty retreat via the side door. He found himself face-to-face with Elvis.

"Thank you very much, Reverend," Elvis drawled. "Thank you very much."

Bibi and the family shook hands with the funeral directors and were then guided out into the condolence lounge. A selection of sweet and savoury foods was available on tables. Urns and everything necessary for self-serve tea, coffee, and fruit juice stood against one wall. There were only a few chairs. People were not encouraged to outstay their welcome.

The family stood by a table with one of the floral tributes, a photograph of Joe, and a condolence book on it. Gradually people gathered in an orderly queue to pay their respects.

"Viv and Tom seem to be the ones holding it all together," Sylvia remarked to Rebecca as they stood in the line-up. The family doesn't seem to know many of these people, do they?"

"I wonder if Elvis got a piece of fruit cake," Rebecca muttered quietly. She and Sylvia began giggling and had to rummage in their handbags to find tissues to stifle their amusement.

"I haven't been to many funerals," Sylvia said as she dabbed at her eyes, "but I think it would be pretty safe to say that this will be one of the most memorable I am likely to attend!"

"Hallelujah and amen!" said Rebecca, suddenly realising their positions in the queue had advanced and she now stood face-to-face with Meg.

Embarrassed for them both, Sylvia dabbed at her eyes, hoping to give the impression of being tearful. Unable to think of something appropriate to say, she hugged Meg.

Meg held on to her firmly and whispered in her ear, "I'm going to sue that damned vicar."

CHAPTER 12

PERTH, WESTERN AUSTRALIA, THURSDAY

"Quickly, girls, please. I need to see Mrs. Bender this morning."
Suzanne had swapped shoes at the last minute and was wiping
off a scuff mark. Jade was standing by the door, ready for departure.

Opal was stuffing her lunchbox into her school bag but couldn't
quite make it fit. "You moved my bag, Pearl. You're supposed to leave
my stuff alone."

"I didn't touch your bag, Opal. Why would I touch your stupid bag?"

"Don't say my bag's stupid. Oh, what's wrong with this stupid bag?"
Opal threw her backpack down onto the floor and stamped her foot.

"You need to empty it. It's got too much in it," Jade said, crossing
her arms. "Mum, we'll be late. You know I like to meet Sophie."

Suzanne was checking out the cash in her purse and replacing it
into her handbag. She hastily went across to Opal and emptied the
schoolbag. There were several pieces of paper and cards scrunched
into balls, discarded rubbish from lunchbox items, a school jumper, a
skipping rope, and two library books.

"No wonder you can't fit things in, Opal. You should tidy your bag
every day when you come home from school." Suzanne picked it up
and tipped everything onto the workbench. Opal returned the jumper,
books, and lunchbox into her bag and slung it over her shoulders, hitting
Pearl as she did so.

"Owww! Mum!"

"Girls, please. We need to go.

Suzanne was silently rehearsing what she should say to Mrs. Bender. She had endured a tortuous night and woken with a stinking headache. It may have been just as well that she was a few minutes later than usual, as all the parents seemed to be returning to their cars. Small groups of children were happily chatting on the veranda. Mrs. Bender was alone in the classroom, accessing the daily roll and the image of the day on the smartboard.

"Mrs. Meadows," greeted Mrs. Bender with a smile.

"Mrs. Bender," Suzanne blurted out. "I must apologise. I can't say how sorry I am, but yesterday, when I was on the cake stall, I was counting the take at the end of the afternoon. We did quite well. Anyway, I realised when I got home that I had accidentally put some of the money into my purse. I-I was changing some smaller notes into fifties. Anyway, this thirty dollars should go into the sales profit. She hurriedly took out her purse and retrieved the folded notes that she had in fact deliberately placed into the pocket of her jeans. She pressed the money into Mrs. Bender's hands. Suzanne's eyes filled with tears. "I am so sorry."

Mrs. Bender looked directly at Suzanne, keeping hold of the money and her hands as she spoke. "The important thing is, Suzanne, that you noticed your … mistake … and put things right. I'm sure it won't happen again. Will it?"

"No. Absolutely not. God, no."

"We all do daft things when we're under pressure. Are you? Under pressure, I mean?"

"No. Just the usual. Like everybody. I'm sorry. I must go. Thank you." Suzanne rushed out of the classroom and extricated a protesting Pearl from underneath the bag bench, talking her along to her room just as the bell sounded.

Mrs. Bender removed a square of coloured notepaper from its neat and tidy cardboard holder, picked up a bright blue felt writing pen, and wrote "Suzanne" on it. She circled it twice and adhered it to the notes of the day section of her daily work pad.

"Good morning, Geoffrey." William smiled pleasantly. "Not at the coalface today?"

"I have a few errands to run. My first appointment cancelled. I wanted to have a word with your seamstress if I could. I've heard she has a creative flair, and I have a proposition."

"Oh, right. You must mean Sylvia. Yes, she is indeed talented." William could almost hear the imaginary "caching" of the now-obsolete cash register. I'm afraid she is on leave currently. In England. A funeral, unfortunately. What did you have in mind, exactly?"

"Well, it would be a rather specific order. I might have to make alternative arrangements. I'm after two Egyptian costumes for a theatrical piece I am putting on with Martin."

"Oh, how lovely." William was about to fudge the details of Sylvia's expected date of return when Crystal, who had been listening in as she was working on the final stages of the curtaining order, with, it had to be said, a fair degree of skill and enthusiasm, spoke up.

"We could do it!"

William looked at Crystal, somewhat taken aback.

"Ruth's good, and she's got me to help with all the basics. Do you wanna look at some patterns? It's, like, fancy dress, is it?" Ruth appeared from the back of the store, where she had been putting the finishing touches on a delicate slightly damaged bridal veil.

"There," said William. "Sylvia will be returning soon, but we can get on with the costumes immediately if time is of the essence."

"Sounds promising." Geoffrey hesitated momentarily. "I tell you what: I'll have a word with Martin. I can't spare the time now, but we'll come back late afternoon to look at possibilities. How's that? I didn't know you still worked here, Ruth. Your reputation is stellar, if I remember correctly!"

Ruth blushed. "I'm sure we can work out something special for you. It will be a pleasure, Geoffrey."

Gratified with Crystal's efforts with the curtain order, now completed and packaged for collection, Ruth felt she had found success with Crystal. The bright pink gum no longer made unwanted appearances. A skirt and black tights replaced black leggings. Sensing Crystal's enthusiasm at the prospect of working on the Egyptian costumes for Geoffrey, Ruth took the opportunity to give Crystal a pep talk. Convincing William that she could cooperate with customers and produce quality work might result in his support of the design course she wanted to do.

Geoffrey had telephoned and arranged to discuss the order during late night shopping hours. "I'm sure we should be able to find something in here." Crystal dragged a large pattern book out from beneath one of the workbenches. Geoffrey had come prepared with some stage magazine photographs. The two of them hit it off immediately.

Ruth didn't work the late night stint, so William removed his jacket and got on with the task of serving customers, accepting that Crystal needed to be giving Geoffrey her full attention. At one point, Martin joined them. He asked whether William would object to his moving behind the counter to have a closer look at the designs. "Oooh, I say. We shall make our mark. I think I shall leave you to it. Can I get coffees for everyone? I might be a while; there's probably a queue."

"Dad, can I come to the park with you and Prince?" Jade asked Ben as she watched him secure the dog's lead.

"Of course, if you want to. What brought this on?" He supposed Jade was trying out the angle of playing sharing and caring daughter to soften him up about the pony club and, inevitably, a pony. She could try, but it wouldn't work. He was sticking to his guns on this one.

"Dunno. I'd like to go to the park with you."

"Okay. You'd better change your shoes, then." Oh God, it couldn't be a boy, could it? Surreptitious arrangements to meet "accidentally"? Ben felt a pang of guilt. There were some questionable thoughts in his head, as it happened.

Walking to the park was enjoyable, though. When Jade was little, Ben adored her. But over time, she seemed to become more and more demanding. To his surprise, Jade chatted about school and how she might try out for the school musical. Sophie, ponies, and clubs didn't rate a mention. When they reached the park, however, Jade grew quieter. Ben was sure she wanted to say something specific. Maybe she had just been warming up and pony talk was imminent. He wasn't going to prompt her.

Ben threw the ball a few times. Prince bounded playfully. Jade found a stray stick. She picked it up, but instead of throwing it for Prince to retrieve it, she began breaking it apart. "Dad," she said. "I'm a bit ..."

"You're a bit what?" *Probably upset because she can't have a pony.*

"Is Mum all right, do you think?" Prince wagged his tail at her, and she threw the stick for him.

"Mum? All right? What do you mean?" This was unexpected. "Has she told you she isn't feeling well or something?"

"No. But there have been a couple of times when ..." Prince bounced back with the short stick, and Jade threw it again. "I thought she had been crying. I was pretty sure she had been crying. She had splashed her face and put on some more make-up, but I could see the blotches on her face."

"Probably she was upset about Opal and Pearl fighting all the time. I mean, it gets on my nerves." Ben laughed awkwardly. "Sometimes I want to bang their heads together."

"No. I don't think so. Both times she had been in the bedroom. I've seen her come out and ..."

Ben waited. "And?"

"I shouldn't do this—it's a bit naughty—but sometimes I sneak into Mum's wardrobe and take out her jewellery. I like to look at it. Mum's got some gorgeous stuff."

"I don't think you need to feel too guilty about that, sweetheart!" Ben was quite relieved. Jade was worried about being caught out. It was quite cute. "Next time ask Mum if you can try them on together. She'd like that, I reckon."

"I don't think there will be a next time, Dad." Prince adopted an obedient posture and sat expectantly in front of them. "When I went in there yesterday, I opened every single drawer of her jewellery case. They were empty. I think all of her jewellery is gone."

Alan drove directly to the airport once the business closed for the day. He felt renewed with confidence. He was sure he had seen Nina at the airport minimart. At first, just having seen her was overwhelming. The realisation that she was in the same state seemed too good to be true. He had to speak to her. Even if nothing could ever come of it, or if he had lost her forever, he had to try.

During the day, Alan had had a brainwave. If he couldn't see her in the store, he would go in and purchase a bunch of flowers, which would probably come with a business card. If not, he could make an excuse of needing to contact them for some reason. He would have a number. Simple.

Arriving at the airport, he made immediately for the coffee shop directly opposite the minimart. He ordered coffee and then proceeded to peruse the rack of loan magazines, hoping he didn't appear furtive. He selected a monthly edition related to model trains. He had no interest in model trains, but it was the best on offer.

He sat, took the lid from his coffee, and opened the illustrated publication.

"Hello, Alan."

He looked up at the woman who had spoken and dropped his long black macchiato in shock.

CHAPTER 13

LONDON, UK, THURSDAY

"Not too heavy on the pickle, thank you, Vivienne." Meg was seated at the table in the kitchen with a cup of coffee made for her by Viv. She had found an unopened packet of breakfast biscuits in the pantry. Having declared them unfit for human consumption, she hastily tore away at the packaging and took a bite. "I can see why people are so impressed with our breakfasts. Is there any fruit, perchance?"

"I'll put a mandarin and a mini Swiss roll in each, okay?" Viv was about to comment on providing them with a school lunchbox when she heard her father and brother coming down the stairs. Tom had prepared to stay for a few nights. It was convenient and enabled him to spend a bit of time with his parents. It took him longer to commute, however, and he would need to leave soon, as he was delivering a lecture at ten that morning.

"So we're trying to cover all bases: environmental, socio-economic, multicultural, non-gender specific. The list goes on. And probably only a few are listening anyway. The internet covers everything. Good morning," he continued genially. "Have a safe trip back."

"Well, it's not going to be an enjoyable trip back. I can't get that ridiculous image of that repulsive Elvis impersonator out of my head. What a disgraceful debacle! Don't waste any time, Tom. I'm telling you I want him sued."

Tom looked awkwardly at his father.

"I could do with a coffee myself." Peter fetched a cup, filled it from the dated but charming coffee pot, and took it to the table. Megan had eaten all the biscuits.

"I don't think Tom is going to have much luck there, love."

"I am not prepared to let this go, Peter! It was a complete and utter fiasco. Highly embarrassing."

Peter bit his tongue. Privately, he was impressed with Joe's Last Stand, as it were. And Joe was his father, not Megan's.

"The priest must have been fulfilling Dad's wishes. Otherwise, he would have been the one footing Elvis's bill, and I can't see that happening, frankly."

"Don't be ridiculous, Peter. If he did come up with it himself, which I don't believe for one minute, he was not of sound mind at the time, and that makes it even worse because that unscrupulous vicar took advantage of him in more ways than one." Megan jabbed her painted fingernail at the tabletop as if counting off the vicar's dishonest deeds.

"We shall have to leave soon." Peter took a few sips of his coffee. It was cold, and it took an effort not to grimace.

"I can't see the vicar before the weekend, I'm afraid. I'll let you know when I've spoken to him." Tom hugged his father and patted his mother's hand. "Sorry, but I must go.

"Viv, what about asking the folks next door to join us for dinner this evening? Sylvia took the trouble to come all this way. Rebecca would be pleased, I'm sure. And we'll all provide company for Bibi. I can be home by four. We can work out food and stuff then, can't we?"

"And that's another thing." Megan tapped the table again. "Poor Bibi. As if she weren't upset enough already, having to endure such a travesty!" She looked at each of them triumphantly, as if congratulating herself on her effective use of the English language.

"Erm—yes. Okay then. Don't worry. I'll get food today if you help me prepare the meal. It's a good idea." Viv avoided her mother's gaze.

Tom made a hasty retreat.

Peter took his coffee cup to the sink. "Would you be ready to leave in fifteen minutes?"

"Please come to dinner, won't you?" Vivienne implored. "I think we've all found this difficult. It was such a shock, losing Joe so suddenly. It didn't seem real somehow, until we were in the church. And Mother is in a stinking mood about the funeral. All of us chatting together would help all of us, I'm sure. Please?"

Sylvia made eye contact with Rebecca. "What do you think, Mum? Do you feel up to going in for a meal next door? Or would you rather just the two of us remain here? You decide. I'm fine either way."

"It's a most generous invitation, Vivienne, if you're sure. What can I bring for dessert?"

"No. Please. We'll do it. Nothing fancy—just good company. Seven o'clock?"

Rebecca rang the doorbell at a minute past seven. Both she and Sylvia were dressed casually in jeans. Rebecca held a bottle of wine, and Sylvia had a box of chocolates. Opening the door, Tom beckoned them into the generously proportioned hallway.

"Thank you for these, although there was no need." Tom relieved them both of their offerings. "Come on through. The quicker I pour you both a drink, the better."

"And we haven't even got to drive home!" Sylvia remarked, hoping she didn't sound too jocular. "Something smells good!" That sounded inappropriate. "The house looks the same as I remember it." Insensitive. *Oh God, please don't let this be one of those occasions when I put my foot in it every time I open my mouth.*

"Red or white, Rebecca?" asked Tom.

"Red, please."

"Me too," Sylvia chirped as she picked up an empty glass and chinked it against another one accidentally.

"Have you had some already?" Tom enquired as he took the glass from her and poured her a measure of red.

"No. No. I've been dry for three days. Shit. I mean …"

"I think the emotional roller coaster we've been on is approaching its rapid descent, Sylvia."

"You're right. And I've just realised I haven't said how sorry I am. Not properly. That's what's making me feel awkward. Can we start again?" Putting down her glass, Sylvia wrapped her arms around Tom and hugged him. "I am very sorry, Tom. Joe was a special man." Tom hugged her back, and then they broke apart. Vivienne came alongside her, and they hugged too. Sylvia expressed her regrets once more. Bibi was seated at the table in her wheelchair. Rebecca had knelt beside her, and the two of them were hugging and wiping away tears. "I know how much you loved each other. Joe is going to be sorely missed by everyone, but especially by you. Remember, I'm next door if you need me or if you want to chat."

"I think we need food!" announced Viv. Both she and Tom started loading up the table with curry, rice, several different pieces of bread, a plate of cold meats, and a salad platter.

"Sit wherever, everyone," Tom instructed. At that very moment, the doorbell rang. Tom laid the serving utensils on the table and went to answer the door. Rebecca sat next to Bibi and asked if she needed an extra cushion.

"May I sit here?" Sylvia asked as she pulled out the chair on the other side of Bibi, placed a napkin on Bibi's lap, and one on her own. "This looks wonderful, doesn't it?"

Tom walked back into the room, closely followed by the Reverend Seaworth, vicar of St Jude's. Everyone fell silent. The vicar flushed scarlet.

"Everyone, allow me to introduce you to Tobias Seaworth, the vicar of St Jude's. You'd remember him from yesterday's funeral, of course. He has kindly agreed to join us for dinner. Vivienne hastily set another place at the table and invited him to sit next to her.

"Wine, Vicar?" asked Tom.

Tobias allowed himself to be persuaded to indulge in a "small glass" of wine and suggested that he might offer thanks.

"Yes, please. Of course." Vivienne presumed she could speak on everyone's behalf.

"Are you a singing family?" the reverend enquired.

"Singing?" Viv's stomach turned summersaults. *Please, God, don't tell me Elvis is hiding somewhere, ready and waiting to offer a rendition of "Ave Maria."*

"Some families like to sing their grace ..."

"Oh, no." Tom handed Tobias his glass of wine. "Just a simple version will suffice."

Everyone was thankful when Tobias sat after a mere sentence-long blessing.

"Start helping yourselves, everybody." Tom allocated the serving utensils to appropriate dishes. "We hope you like curry—it's quite mild—and there are two kinds of rice ..."

The doorbell rang again. "Goodness," said Vivienne. She shook her head as Tom went to move. "I'll get it. I hope it's not Jehovah's Witnesses!" She laughed and then caught sight of the vicar's pursed lips. "I mean ..." She looked at Tom, silently begging him to begin a discussion that had nothing to do with funerals, religion, Elvis Presley, or lawyers.

"Rebecca. We don't get to see you nearly often enough, do we? Even though you do only live next door. You are working, aren't you? You'll have to remind me, I'm afraid."

Rebecca was tearing off a piece of crusty bread and looking around for the butter. "Yes. I'm working for ..." She saw Viv come back into the room, looking more embarrassed than she did when she left it. A man followed her in, grinning rather sheepishly. Rebecca dropped the bread back into the basket from whence it came, as well as the butter knife, which clattered noisily onto her plate and then fell to the floor.

"Gerry?" Rebecca was stunned. "Gerry. What in the blazes?"

"Dad? Oh my God." Sylvia burst into tears and covered her face with her napkin.

"I'm sorry. I read Joe's death notice in the paper, and I wanted to pay my respects."

"I've asked Gerry to stay for dinner," Vivienne said. "There's plenty of food."

CHAPTER 14

Thankfully, most of Alan's spilt coffee was soaked up by a local paper conveniently left on the table by a previous occupant. Alan's gut reaction had been to grab the cup and set it upright. Nina rushed forward, pulled copious paper napkins from their receptacle, and wiped up any liquid before it ran to the floor. The cafe assistant, who was engaged in wiping the tables anyway, cleared up any remaining spillage without comment.

"Sorry," said Alan to the rather sullen and tired-looking woman.

"Thank you," said Nina.

Alan looked at the magazine, liberally sprayed with coffee, and put it in the bin.

"Could we ... erm ...?"

"Walk?" said Nina.

Both of them seemed afraid to say more. It was as if a spell would break if either spoke. Alan spied an unoccupied bench a short distance from the minimart. He gestured towards it, inviting Nina to sit.

"I shall have to finish checking the flowers. I was going to pick up a smoothie."

"Don't go. Please, Nina. Don't go."

"Why are you here, Alan? Are you meeting someone?"

"Can I wait, Nina? For you, I mean. Wait here for you?"

"I don't think that's a good idea." Alan's heart sank. "I've got an hour and a half to go. Security will think you're up to no good." She smiled at him and turned to leave. He wanted to stop her from walking away. He tried to say something to keep her there, but the words caught in his throat. He watched her back as she moved away from him. He felt desperate.

Then she turned and pulled something out of her pocket. She walked back to Alan and handed him a card. The front of the card was pink, edged with small flowers, and bore the name Bouquets. The reverse side listed floral services, a website, and a telephone number.

Ben deliberately waited until he heard the shower running. Suzanne always took a shower before they went to bed. He went into the spacious walk-in wardrobe. Suzanne's jewellery case, located within an underwear drawer, was partially hidden beneath copious pairs of knickers, presumably to confuse burglars, Ben thought wryly. He had to lift the case out to open it properly. Suzanne wouldn't take long. Placing the box on the clothes chest as quietly as possible, he lifted the lid. The three gold necklaces bought for her following the girls' births were there. Gingerly he opened the drawers beneath, one by one. Everything seemed to be in place. The shower stopped. He quickly returned the jewellery case to its spot, covered it again with the knickers, and made his way downstairs. Jade was mistaken.

Suzanne was liberally soaping herself up with a new shower gel. It had to stop. She could hardly believe how the incident with the cake stall had come about. But she had put it right.

After the morning school run, Suzanne had driven straight around to her mother's place and told her everything. The gambling, the clothing allowances, the Christmas fund. Pawning the jewellery and taking the money from the stall. She thought she would die of shame.

She sobbed and sobbed. Suzanne's mother listened to everything and then disappeared for a few moments. She came back dressed in one of her best outfits and carrying her favourite handbag.

"Get into the car, Suzanne. We're going to pick up every bit of that jewellery." Suzanne dried her eyes and stared at her mother. "We'll take my car. You can fix up your face while I'm driving. You'll have to direct me to the pawnshop—I have no idea where it is. Come on," she ordered crisply.

Someone was smiling on her. Usually items of high quality were kept to one side until they were checked against any stolen goods notifications sent out by police and insurance companies and verified as being genuinely saleable. The process could take several days.

"Good morning," said Suzanne's mother brightly. "I'm here to redeem several items of jewellery brought into your store a few days ago. There has been a misunderstanding, entirely down to me, but I won't bore you with the details. I do hope they are as yet unsold. I realise I may need to speak with the manager in the circumstances."

"I see. Did you retain the duplicate sales docket? It has a sales number on it."

"Yes." Suzanne took out her purse and retrieved the docket. Her hands were trembling. It was amazing that she hadn't thrown it away. She handed it to the store assistant, who took it through to the back of the store. She returned a few minutes later with a tray of items.

"You are most fortunate, madam. These pieces were due to go out today." Setting the tray on the counter and laying the docket beside it, she began checking the list. "If you would identify them, please, dear?"

Suzanne didn't argue. "That's twelve in all."

"Wonderful." Suzanne's mother beamed. "If you would kindly let me know how much I owe?"

"Of course," said the shop assistant. "May I see your driving licences, please?"

LONDON, THURSDAY

Vivienne realised as soon as Gerry walked in behind her that she had made a colossal mistake. She hadn't been thinking straight. Now it was too late. Both Rebecca and Sylvia confronted Gerry, and now they were faced with him. Mind you, could she have refused him entry? Hardly. But she could have asked him to wait and warned them.

Gerry, however, seemed very bright and breezy. "Hello, Rebecca. I did call in next door, but when I got no response, I thought I'd try here. Nice to see you, love. You're looking well, I must say. Sylvia! I thought you were in Australia! What a turn out, eh? Have you got a hug for your old dad?"

Gerry looked around him at all the dumbstruck faces. Suddenly, he seemed to notice the awkwardness. "Shall I come back tomorrow?"

Bibi was the first to break the silence. "Gerry Bourne, as I live and breathe. You have always been the absolute master of the ill-timed moment, but this one just about takes the cake. If Joe were here, he would pronounce you a complete and utter moron and then offer you a drink. Rebecca, shall we throw him out on your behalf? Sylvia, do you want him kicked from here to next week?"

"Sylvia, are you happy for your father to stay?" Rebecca ventured.

"I guess we could give him ten minutes, half an hour at the most. Crazy idiot. Just excuse me for a moment, everybody." Sylvia located her handbag and headed for the bathroom to repair her face. She would have to have several more glasses before she hugged the stupid idiot, she told herself.

On her return, she found Gerry seated next to the vicar with a plate of food and a glass of wine in front of him. The vicar seemed to have claimed an attentive audience.

"Yes, we have good attendance numbers at St Jude's. We are quite heavily involved in the community. Joe and I met through one of our groups. We became quite good friends. On that note, I failed to explain my visit this evening. The purpose of my visit is twofold. Firstly, I have a copy of Joe's eulogy as well as the 'musical performance.'" He smiled rather indulgently, removed a DVD from his inside jacket pocket, and placed it on the table. "Secondly, I always try to make a point of visiting the bereaved following a funeral. You would be amazed at how often I discover people sitting alone, with no one to comfort them. It is most gratifying to see that, in your case, you are all supporting one another at a difficult time."

"Performance?" Gerry quizzed.

"Erm, yes." Tom tore off another piece of bread and requested that the butter be moved farther down the table. "Joe chose to deliver his eulogy. Reverend, when did Joe record that message?"

"Well, that is one of the remarkable things about it. It was only one month ago, almost to the day. It's not that unusual for people to have a sense of their time on this earth drawing to a close. They tend not to share those thoughts with loved ones, for obvious reasons. He asked me to record his thoughts, and I did so. He was sure of what he wanted to say. It was written down, but I remember being struck by the fact that he hardly referred to it at all. He spoke from the heart. On the bottom of the paper, he had written, 'Get me, Elvis!' I asked what he meant, and he said, "When I go, I want the place to be moving and shaking. He noted down the name and details of his solicitor. Much to my surprise, when I contacted them, they confirmed that a generous amount of money had been set aside for the hiring of an impersonator. If all else failed, then YouTube would have to suffice. Any remaining money was to go to St Jude's. It's quite an incredible story, isn't it?"

"You mean that Joe had Elvis performing at his funeral? Ha ha!" Gerry slapped his leg several times. "And nobody knew? The sly old devil, going out with a bang!"

"Do you still have the written instructions?" Tom asked, refreshing everybody's wine glasses.

"Absolutely." The reverend placed his hand over his glass and shook his head. "No more, thank you. And of course, the solicitor will have kept his copy."

Having spent the last few years living in Australia, Sylvia had not seen her father for some time. She could not deny, however, as the evening wore on, that she was pleased to see him. As was, she observed, her mother.

Rebecca had fallen head over heels for Gerry. They had met at a dance. She had gone along with a friend who had just completed an eight-week dance course, culminating in a ball at which the enthusiastic fledglings were encouraged to showcase their skills. Of course, more seasoned dancers were also there, making it quite evident that the recent recipients of a city ballroom beginner's certificate were merely at the start of their dance journey, and many improvements and advancements would result if they attended the second and third courses. The tutors, of whom Gerry was one, gave some exhibition dances.

As she learned to sweep across the dance floor, Gerry swept Rebecca off her feet. He was very attentive, but it took three complete courses for him to ask her out eventually. He took her to a more sophisticated ballroom and danced with her alone. When Gerry finally proposed, Rebecca asked no questions, made no demands. She said yes, and they moved into the small flat that was to become home for Rebecca.

Money was not plentiful. Gerry worked in a few bars to supplement his income from dance classes, and Rebecca worked from home as a seamstress. When Sylvia came along, Gerry suggested he expand the dance classes to cover several other suburbs and even take in a couple of country towns. Staying overnight made more sense economically, he explained. Gradually his trips home became far less frequent. When he was home, he lavished Rebecca and Sylvia with loving kindness and bonhomie. Gerry always ensured that he paid the rent, and this rather bizarre arrangement continued, unquestioned.

"Let's move the furniture back a bit," Gerry suggested, once the meal appeared to be over. "Can you find us some dance music, Viv?"

Tom dutifully found himself assisting in moving the furniture, and Viv located some music. Sylvia and Rebecca cleared the table. The vicar excused himself and bade them all farewell. Gerry had the knack of getting everyone to do his bidding before they even realised they were doing it. When Rebecca and Sylvia came back into the room, Gerry grabbed one hand of each of them and began to rock and roll with both of them at one time, just as he had when Sylvia was in her teens. Tom took hold of Bibi's wheelchair and jigged about with it in time to the music. He then settled her in a corner so that she wouldn't get jostled around.

"You're doing backup vocals, Bibi!" Tom laughed.

Tom and Viv paired and took up the rock and roll beat. After a while, the two men swapped places. They all sang and danced until the CD ended, when they all collapsed, exhausted. Viv and Tom went to make coffee.

"So, Bibi, that old dog had his way with the send-off then? I wish I could've been there to see it."

"We've got a recording."

"Recording? Oh, yes, of course. The vicar brought it around. Well, I'll be. Any chance we could—?"

"Watch it? I don't see why not." Gerry's zest for life enthralled Bibi. His sense of fun was incredibly infectious, despite his reprehensible attitude towards marriage and responsibility.

They watched the DVD twice and then decided to call it a night. Sylvia was intrigued to see what would happen next. She, Rebecca, and Gerry left together and, without preamble, walked through the front door of the flat. Rebecca and Gerry kissed Sylvia goodnight and then went through to Rebecca's bedroom.

Well, I'll be, thought Sylvia.

In the morning, Gerry had gone.

CHAPTER 15

"So that's it, boss," Nev said, as he closed the maintenance book. "Did that couple get back to you about the camper van?"

"Oh, erm, no," Alan stalled. He walked around a well-kept Honda and inspected the windscreen wipers critically.

"It's just that Schubert needs to visit his mob. Deal with a few things, you know? He was wonderin' if he could use it for a bit. I said I'd have to ask you."

"Yes. That would be fine. Good. Wipers are good." Alan was relieved.

The euphoria Alan had felt from the previous evening had evaporated somewhat, as he didn't know what his next move should be. If Nina didn't want to see him, she wouldn't have given him the card. But it wasn't her mobile number. Nina probably wouldn't answer the phone. And if she did, what would he say? Asking her for a date would be ridiculous. He wanted to talk. Actually, they needn't even speak. Just seeing her, being with her, would be … God. Was he a stalker? He knew the camper van thing was illogical, as well as reading the horoscope. He had to put the ball back into her court in a way that wasn't threatening. Not that he was a threat. What was he, exactly?

Robert had managed to secure two sales at virtually the same time. Two friends who up until now had shared accommodation and a car had decided that independence on the road was now a requirement. They would trade in the shared vehicle and purchase one each. Robert took the trouble to explain procedures and paperwork to Delvine. Alan had more time on his hands and was able to work on promotions and advertising. It was paying off too.

"Excuse me for saying," Delvine ventured, "but I think you could organise your digital records more effectively. Would you like me to see what I can do with them?"

"Sounds good. I'll have to check with the boss, of course." He looked at Alan expectantly, but he hadn't been listening. "Hey, boss, are you all right with that?"

"With what?"

"With Delvine sorting out our digital records."

"Yes, yes. Of course. No worries."

Robert hesitated, as he wasn't quite sure whether Alan was listening. Alan took no notice, however.

"Guess that's okay, then!" Robert grinned. He moved a little closer to Delvine and dropped his voice, just in case Alan suddenly joined the land of the attentive. "Would you be interested in … having a drink sometime?"

Delvine settled herself behind the main computer screen. "Potential," she said, nodding in the direction of the yard. A car was pulling in. Robert moved towards the door.

"Maybe," Delvine said. "Sometime."

Suzanne had been given strict instructions by her mother, Gina, as to what she should do on Friday once she had finished the laundry. She was to begin keeping a diary—at the front, a confession. She should omit nothing. Then she was to write a promise to herself that she would never let this happen again. There was to be an entry every day. If she felt the urge to gamble, she had to write it down in the diary. She could phone her mother and talk to her whenever necessary.

Gina was blaming herself for this turn of events. Frank had indulged Suzanne to a ridiculous degree, and she had gone along with it. The only time she had stood against him was when he had supported Suzanne's idea of taking up art and design at the local technical college. Gina knew that was no way to go about acquiring a higher-than-average income. Suzanne needed to be admired and seen in all the right circles, modelling classes. That was the way to go. Gina felt sure that Suzanne would be the worthy recipient of a contract. Who knew where it would eventually lead? At the least, modelling should bring her into contact with eligible men. Admittedly, a car salesman didn't entirely fall within the calibre she had envisaged. Nonetheless, Ben was hard-working and successful.

She had no idea where the diary strategy originated, probably a magazine in a waiting room somewhere. Nor did she know whether it would prove useful, but she had to suggest something. Suzanne wasn't kept short of money; she was sure of that. Was it boredom? Too much time on her hands?

The next instruction was to make a list of the things she liked doing, other than domestic chores. Gina would help Suzanne set up a hobby room.

Having complied with the confession and the promise, Suzanne found herself staring at a blank page. Blank page, empty mind. She began doodling with her pen. It was noon. She was supposed to phone her mother at one with a list of potential time fillers. The ink grew denser in colour as the doodling gradually spread across the page. It split where she had angrily scribbled circles and lines over and over, interspersing and colliding. Eventually, the page ripped in two. She tore out the scraps and threw them into the bin. The sheet beneath was marked and pitted. Across it, she scrawled, "I hate my stupid bloody self." She then threw the diary at the wall. It bounced off the wall and landed on the treadmill. Suzanne kicked it off, stood on the tread mat, and started up the machine. The rhythm pounded through her feet and up to her brain as she upped the speed of her walking pace.

At twenty, Suzanne had been a beauty consultant at Feinnes Department store in the city. Shortly after meeting Ben, she had fallen pregnant. He was already on the road to success. He also knew Suzanne's father was well connected and well off. There was no question of their not marrying. She need not work, she boasted to her colleagues in her last few weeks of employment. She tried to picture the exquisitely made-up faces of the girls she had worked alongside fourteen years ago. Struggling to bring them to mind, she slowed the machine down and came to a halt. It suddenly dawned on her. She didn't have a single real friend.

Jade sipped from her water bottle. She was nervous, yes, but she knew she was doing okay in the first round of the auditions. The older students made up the main cast. This week's double-sport period was set aside for those who wanted to audition for the chorus. Anyone who chose to audition got the chance.

"And … five, six, seven, eight." The twelve hopefuls slid and sashayed their way through the relatively short dance routine designed to identify those who could actually dance and remember routine steps as well as take the whole thing seriously. There was no tolerance for time wasters. One staff member was calling the steps and dancing with them; another two were making notes. Rachel, along with two senior boys, had been designated sound technicians. Most chaplains found that becoming involved with student activities made their jobs so much easier. They got to know them and developed a rapport.

"Good, good. Well done, everybody. Next group, please." Jade put down her water bottle and took her place. She wanted this so badly that it almost hurt.

"This time we're going with the music. Don't rush it. Thank you, Rachel." The dance instructor gave Rachel a thumbs up for the music to begin. "And … five, six, seven, eight."

Summer lovin' had me a blast.

Rachel was thrilled to see the passion of the staff and the students as they put their heart and soul into this. A good number of students would have the chance to perform. Two complete casts were chosen to cover six performances over two weeks. Backup singers boosted the vocals on either side of the stage, and there was plenty of scope for stagehands and so on. Some of the students were standing out. Jade was one of them.

Jade puzzled Rachel. There tended to be distinct groups towards which the students gravitated. There were the academics, the sports obsessed, and the troublemakers (who took up a good deal of her time). Then there was a group with affluent parents who had the best of everything and would mostly succeed because of their social status. Jade appeared to be on the fringe of this group when hanging around with Sophie. But she didn't quite belong. The mid-ways, as Rachel privately named them, were from stable, dependable families with their own struggles and issues who mostly made the best of things. Jade didn't seem to belong there either.

Jade kept going over her dad's calm reassurance earlier that day. The jewellery was where it should be. He could only think that her mum was reorganising or was having it cleaned, perhaps.

"But why would she cry? Why don't you know?"

Ben seemed unable to answer. He put his fingers to his lips and cautioned her to hush. "Grown-ups don't always tell each other everything, sweetheart. I'm sure your mum's fine."

Rachel smiled encouragingly at Jade as the first round of auditions closed off and the students began to exit the hall. Jade took several generous gulps from her water bottle and then approached the sound desk.

"Chaplain Rachel, could I come and see you about something?"

Rachel nodded as she thanked the boys for their assistance with the sound and confirmed their attendance for the following Monday. The packing away was almost complete. Jade put her water bottle away and slipped on her backpack.

"I've got ten minutes now before a meeting. Or would you sooner make it next week? Final dance auditions on Monday. Are you nervous about that? You didn't seem nervous."

"Have you heard about good secrets and bad secrets?" Jade pulled her hair out of its ponytail, ran her fingers through it, and threaded it through the black hair elastic again.

Rachel's stomach turned. Oh no. She was familiar with the Pro Protection Program used by most schools to educate students and parents about the prevention of abuse in its multiple guises. Recognising the danger signs before anything occurred was crucial. Safe and unsafe secrets formed part of the health curriculum that began in primary classes.

"Yes." Rachel turned the key in the lock of the sound equipment cupboard and gave Jade her full attention. "Have you been asked to keep a secret that you feel uncomfortable with, Jade?"

Jade related how she had sometimes tried on her mother's jewellery and then discovered that it was missing and how her mum had been crying and covering it up. About her dad not seeming bothered because the missing items had turned up again and claiming that grown-ups kept secrets all the time.

"Things that strike us as odd often do turn out to have innocent explanations, as your dad says. What is it that's worrying you the most about it all?"

"It's all my fault," Jade blurted out. "I wanted a pony. Well, I thought I wanted a pony, but I didn't really. Sophie's got a pony, and she belongs to the pony club. But I don't like horses much. They are a bit smelly. A lot smelly. Why can't I be friends with Sophie and not have a pony? Anyway, a pony must cost heaps, and then there are those clothes—helmets and stuff. Mum goes on about it, and I know if I tell her that's not what I want anymore, she'll blame Dad because he said there's no way I'm getting a pony, and I think it's making them fight, and I think—"

Rachel waited. "You think …?"

"We're running out of money."

CHAPTER 16

PERTH, WESTERN AUSTRALIA, FRIDAY

"It's our assembly next week." Opal clambered into the back of the car and buckled up. "I know what I want to do …"

Pearl followed her in but caught her shoe in the floor mat of the vehicle, causing her to stumble and bump into Opal's elbow. "Owww! You hit me with your stupid elbow, Opal. Mum!"

"I didn't hit you. You fell into the car. Mum, I want to—"

"No, I didn't. You made me fall over, and you hit me with your stupid elbow."

"Be quiet, Pearl. I need to tell Mum about our assembly. Mum, we have to—"

"Don't tell me to be quiet. Who cares about your stupid assembly? Owww. Mum!"

Jade looked across at her mother. She usually walked to the primary school car park at the end of the afternoon and met her mother and sisters there. Suzanne didn't look upset, but she seemed oblivious to the ructions in the back of the car.

"For goodness' sake!" Jade slammed the car door shut and pulled at her seat belt. "I must have the worst sisters."

Suzanne started the engine and began backing out of the parking spot. Someone hooted at her, and she hit the brake.

"You're the worst sister, Jade. Worst sister, worst sister," Pearl chanted.

"Shut up!" Jade yelled. She looked appealingly at her mother.

"Girls, stop it, please. I need to concentrate." Suzanne scanned in every direction.

"It's not *me*. You two make me sick. Why do you have to fight about *everything*?" Jade realised that she had caught her seat belt in the door. Pulling it open hastily, she lost her grip. The door swung wide and hit the car door on her left. The driving seat was occupied by a middle-aged man who closed his eyes and shook his head. Jade sat motionless, staring at the driver of the other car. He pointed his finger jerkily at the door, indicating that she needed to pull the door closed.

"Oh God, Jade." Suzanne unbuckled her seat belt and moved to get out of the car. A woman of rather generous proportions blocking her exit hindered her, however. The woman was holding a conversation with presumably, if looks were anything to go by, her adult daughter, who seemed in no hurry to load three children in the back of a station wagon, collecting a backpack from each as she negotiated manoeuvres. Suzanne rapped her knuckles on the car window. "Excuse me, please." On receiving no response, she used the palm of her hand and considerably more force. "Excuse me!" The owner of the large buttocks shifted awkwardly and turned towards Suzanne, who had opened the door as far as she could.

"Hang on, love. Won't be a sec." Mother and grandmother installed the children, along with their backpacks, into the car before clearing the space between bays, allowing Suzanne to get out of her car.

Suzanne quickly moved around to the passenger side. "Goodness, I'm so sorry." She closed the car door on Jade's behalf to reveal a large gash in the paintwork of the other vehicle. "Oh my goodness."

The man got out of his car. "I was only doing my son a favour. I don't normally do this—pick up the kids. Oh glory be. It's his car and all." He surveyed the damage ruefully.

"We need to exchange insurance details." Suzanne handed over Ben's business card. "My husband works in cars. He can get it fixed in his workshop if you'd rather. It's up to you. I'm very, very sorry."

By the time all the necessary information, including photographs, had been exchanged, the gentleman in question had fully taken in Suzanne's appearance. She was an attractive woman. She was also stressed. He wouldn't have minded offering a little physical comfort but merely said, "These things happen. Car parks are one of the worst places, you know. I'll contact you soon."

"Nina Meadows?" Nina looked up, surprised. She saw the logo of an expensive delivery service on a uniform pocket. They dealt with gourmet foods and surprise weekend packages, as well as late delivery runs for the right price. "Flowers for the florist, it would appear," he said pleasantly, handing Nina a boxed arrangement. Confused, she located the small card. It opened to reveal an email address and the name Alan.

The more Nina thought about it, the more confused she became about what she should do. Did she still have feelings for Alan? Definitely. She had mistreated him. He at least deserved an explanation. Or would that make everything worse? He might hate her and be driven to take extreme measures. Or he might be so desperate to have her back in his life that he would forgive her anything. Her guilt would hang over them like the proverbial sword of Damocles, ready to destroy them both.

Ben returned his phone to his jeans pocket. He had been speaking to Mr. Forsythe regarding the damage to his car—or, to be more precise, his son's car. "You need to take greater care, Jade. Anything to do with cars tends to be expensive. The car door on your side was damaged too."

"It wasn't my fault!" Jade yelled. "There wasn't enough room, and Opal and Pearl were fighting; anyway, it was an accident."

"I realise it was an accident, Jade. I'm not blaming you. These things happen. I'm just saying we all need to take care."

Pearl rushed through into the kitchen, squealing as she ran. Opal was running after her. "Give that to me, Pearl! Mum said I could have it. I need it for my assembly."

"I'm the one who's got it. You can't have it," Pearl chanted in a sing-song voice. She appeared to be clinging on to a screwed-up white dress with both hands. Opal grabbed it and pulled it towards her. There was a ripping sound as Pearl wrestled it from Opal's grasp. Quickly turning, she moved to the other side of the workbench and shoved it into the waste bin. "Ha, all gone." Pearl was triumphant.

"Aaahhhh, Dad!" Opal screeched. "Mum said I could have that dress, and Pearl has ruined it! I hate you, Pearl. I hate you. Dad!"

Ben pulled the dress out of the bin and gave it to Opal. Stained material and ripped stitches resulted in tears.

"Pearl! What on earth has gotten into you? Get to your room." Ben pointed. "Now!"

Pearl laughed. "It's only a stupid old dress. Who cares?"

"*Pearl, stop it!*" Ben thought for a moment. "Opal, take the dress to your mum and see if it can be repaired. Pearl, no allowance money for you for … I don't know how long. I'm taking everything out of your allowance for being so horrible to your sister. Now get to your room." Pearl stomped off and poked her tongue out at Opal. Opal returned the gesture and followed the sound of the vacuum in search of Suzanne.

"Bloody kids." Ben took the dog's lead down from the fancy ironwork coat hooks on the wall and whistled for Prince. He stood in the doorway of the lounge room. Suzanne was inspecting the stitching on the dress; Opal was crying. Pearl was dancing and singing behind the sofa.

"Pearl, I told you to go to your room! *Go!*"

"Mum, it was an accident. I didn't mean to," Pearl whined.

"I know. I can redo the stitching and soak it in stain remover. It should be fine. Put it on top of the washing machine, Opal, and I'll see to it later."

"Suzanne, it wasn't an accident. Pearl was horrible. Go to your room!" Ben was red in the face and took two steps towards Pearl. She dodged out of the way quickly and ran through the door.

"I want every bit of money taken out of her account. She's going to give it to me in cash, and she's not getting any more money until I *bloody well say so*! I'm taking Prince to the park. I want that money when I come back." On hearing Prince scuffling in anticipation, he turned to leave. "And," he added, "she can write a letter of apology to her sister." He closed his eyes briefly to calm himself. She heard the door slam as he left.

Suzanne paled. It was unusual for Ben to raise his voice or use coarse language with the girls. He must have been incensed. But the money was of more significant concern. There was nothing in any of the accounts, except for Ben's. Her card was maxed out. The money from the jewellery sale went on living expenses up until the next pay. She had vowed to have it all sorted by Christmas. What was she going to do?

Jade was becoming convinced that she was right. Her mum had probably tried selling her jewellery (although she might have changed her mind) and was giving her old clothes to Opal. They had never worn second-hand clothes. Was her dad using Pearl's allowance to help pay for the damaged cars? Were they going to be poor, like refugees?

Jade hadn't revisited her mother's jewellery box since Ben had told her that nothing was missing. She knew there had been no mistake on her part. She heard Suzanne turn off the vacuum and accompany Opal to the laundry to examine the dress. While Suzanne was busy with the two younger girls, Jade decided to put her mind at rest and check that the jewellery was indeed still there. Lifting out the box from the drawer, she was surprised to discover a book beneath it. That wasn't there before. A diary. Strictly private. No one had the right to read another person's diary.

"I promise you," Suzanne whispered urgently to her mother on the phone a little later, "I had it all planned to be put right by Christmas.

I don't have the cash now to give to Ben. Please help me, Mum!" She was speaking from the garden, having insisted that Opal and Pearl sit on opposite sides of the TV room and watch a movie from beginning to end. If they fought, they would not be going to Naomi's birthday party next weekend.

"When Ben comes home from the park, I'll say I have to go out to get some angel hair pasta or something and withdraw Pearl's money from the ATM, but I'll come to you. Do you have two hundred to spare?"

"I always have some cash. Suzanne, this *must* stop."

"I know. It will. It has! I haven't done it for ages. I don't have any cash until payday. I think Ben's insisting on Pearl seeing the cash removed from her account to make it more meaningful."

After speaking to Gina, Suzanne felt a little calmer. There would be money in her account on Monday. She would be all right then. Oh God, how would she pay for the pasta? Did she have anything in her purse at all? She grabbed her handbag and quickly checked. There was less than a dollar.

"Jade honey, do you have any of your canteen allowance left? I, erm, need to buy some angel hair pasta, and I'm all out of cash."

"No. Well, I've got fifty cents left, I think. Isn't it payday on Monday?" Jade couldn't remember her mother ever running out of food supplies.

"Of course. Yes, of course. If I have to use my card, it won't matter," Suzanne lied.

CHAPTER 17

LONDON, UK, SATURDAY

"I think if one of us has the vacuum, one has the polish and duster, and the other has the cloth and spray, we could go through each room one at a time and have the place sparkling in a couple of hours." Vivienne had suggested they all work together to give Bibi's place a thorough once-over. "If we work in the same room, we can chat as we go."

"Brilliant," said Sylvia from the inside the broom cupboard under the stairs. Sylvia was pleased with the distraction of housework for a while. She had spent a restless night playing out scenarios in her mind of birthdays and Christmases with and without her father. There was always a present, but often no presence. She recalled times when she would return from school and unexpectedly find him there with Rebecca. He had taught her to dance and once taken her out to buy a pair of red shoes. When he was there, she felt so special. But most of the time he was absent.

Tom was outside cutting the grass and tidying the flower beds.

"What about me?" Bibi asked. "I can't just sit here feeling useless!"

"You don't need the wheelchair all the time, but you mustn't rush things. Anyway, I have just the job for you. Use my iPad and look up some tourist activities for next week. Let's make the most of this enforced labour camp experience, shall we? Can I have the duster? I hate vacuums." Viv placed her iPad, a pencil, and some sticky notes on the table. Rebecca assisted with Bibi's move from the sofa.

"How come you're so techno-literate, Bibi?" Sylvia was experimenting with attaching various hoses and accoutrements to the vacuum. "I'm impressed."

"Tom got Joe and me onto it. He said it's important to keep up with these things—plus we have a bit of fun with the games. Or, I should say, we did." Bibi snuffled a little. Rebecca placed a box of tissues from the dresser in front of her and squeezed her shoulder.

"You can still do those things, Bibi. You'll see. Shall we start in here?"

Before long, the three of them were working companionably in the main living area of the house. Bibi was absorbed in her searches and making notes.

"By the way ..." Bibi stuck a bright yellow sticky note to the table. "Thank you so much for the other night. It was wonderful having some company. I've had enough of moping for the moment. Rebecca and Sylvia, tell me to butt out if you'd rather, but the way you both accommodated Gerry was so—"

"Bloody weird!" Sylvia threw up her hands dramatically and turned off the vacuum. "You've got to admit its bloody weird, haven't you?" Sylvia dropped the hose with a clatter and grabbed some tissues from the box in front of Bibi. She wiped at her eyes exasperatedly. "It can't just be me who finds the situation crazy, right?"

"I shouldn't have mentioned it. Sorry."

"No, that's the thing. It was only last night that I thought about how weird it is. It always has been. Right from when I started school, my dad has worked away and just turned up whenever. And nobody says a thing. He might stay two hours or two days, and then he's gone till the next time—for months and months. And nobody says *anything*!"

Rebecca put down the spray bottle and cloth. She held her arms out to Sylvia. Rather than go to her mother, though, Sylvia sank to the floor. "What's wrong with him? What's wrong with us? Why does he have to keep leaving? And why do we have to let him, you know, breeze in and be the life and soul of the party and then go? Mum, why do you let him do that?"

The back door opened. "Ready for a cuppa?" Tom called out. He walked into the room and cast his eyes over the stunned group of women. "Ah. Bad timing?"

Perth, West Australia, Saturday

Matthew persuaded the girls to go into town sooner rather than later. He assured them that he could have the walls painted within two hours before leaving for his shift. On their return, they were gratified to see fresh primrose-yellow walls. The furniture was in the centre of the room. The cot was put together, probably with the help of Tim from next door, Rachel thought. That left them with hanging the curtains, cleaning out the clothes chest, and furnishing it with baby needs. Rachel wanted to double wash the newly purchased bedding before being used. The weather was fine, so she saw to that while Delvine made them a sandwich and a cuppa. The linen was hung out to dry in the sun by the time they were ready to tackle the curtains.

A friend had passed on the cot and the chest of drawers. Second-hand but in excellent condition, both were painted white and complemented the yellow nursery walls and white doors and skirting that featured throughout the whole house.

"What had you planned on doing with this?" Delvine was examining a plain wooden table included with the other pieces of furniture.

"We were given that when we first moved in. We stood the TV on it. I guess that could be the changing table."

"It could. Or," Delvine ventured, "just an idea, but the two white bookcases in my room could stand back to back. They'd be the right height for nappy changing. All the nappies and stuff could go on the shelves. I'd have the table as a desk, with a couple of book baskets. What do you think?"

"Oh. Very *Reno Rave*, I must say!" Rachel was referring to the popular current TV program that promoted revamping and reusing rather than continually buying new. "I think that's a great idea, if you don't mind."

"I know how to move stuff," Delvine said as she disappeared into the bathroom and returned with a large towel. "That might be the one useful thing to come out of my relationship with Johnny. You put a mat or whatever underneath what you are moving and drag it. Watch me." Sure enough, Delvine had all three furniture pieces successfully relocated reasonably quickly. The chest of drawers was cleaned out and moved to its rightful place, along with the cot. One of the two chairs that accompanied the table sat beside the cot and the other tucked under the makeshift desk assigned to Delvine's room. The two-tone green curtains were then hung over the window.

"I'm going to lie down and rest for a bit, and then I'm going to put all the clothes and baby care things where they belong. Dee, it's a bit rude, I know, but could I do that by myself? It's a bit special."

"Absolutely." Delvine hugged Rachel warmly. "I'll drive down to the local el cheapo store and get myself some baskets for books, okay?"

Rachel dozed for a bit. When she woke, excitement overcame her. The baby room would look lovely when Matthew came home. The bedding was dry, so she brought it inside. That morning saw them heading for the baby superstore in search of the items needed to complete the nursery. However, the designs on offer were too flashy. Rachel wanted a quieter look. They passed by a children's clothing store advertising a closing-down sale. Rachel wondered sadly if the superstore was responsible for the smaller store's demise. They had baby supplies at the back. There they found a whole range of matching bedding along with a change mat and a hanging mobile. There were bargain baskets of nappies, wipes, creams, and lotions. The assistant drew their attention to some clothing items at half price. They returned home laden with good buys. Rachel's mother was providing the bassinet, and Matthew's widowed father, opting out of baby shopping because he "wouldn't have a clue," had told Matthew that he would put money into an account for them to buy whatever they still needed when the time was imminent.

While Rachel organised the drawers, cupboards, and shelves, she felt quite teary. Mathew was such a good man. His mum had died when he was in his late teens. He was so keen to begin a family of his own. They had chosen not to know the sex of the baby. Rachel was grateful to have Delvine around. She was like the sister she had never had.

A short while later, Delvine had returned with a set of baskets, one large and two small, as well as a tufted rag rug in shades of brown and orange. "For the floor. What do you think?" Delvine spread it out with her arms outstretched, waiting for a reaction.

"In your room? Rachel asked, feeling the softness of the materials between her fingers.

"It could," Delvine responded. "But if you like it, it could go here." She laid the rug out on the floor.

"I love it!" Rachel enthused.

"I've got one more thing in the car." Rachel followed her out. She opened up the boot and dragged out a cork pin-up board. "I thought you could pin up pictures and poems and stuff, and then Fatso's paintings can go on it!"

"It's just perfect, Dee. Thank you so much."

"Wait until you hear the story. It's so you, Rachel. I was thinking that I'd try the charity shop first. I pulled up in the car park next to a woman with a loaded boot. I offered to help. She had the book baskets, the rug, and the pin-up board amongst all her stuff, so she said I could take them if I wanted. I got them for *free*!" They carried the board inside and hung it straight up onto the wall.

"Would you believe we've already got two hooks in the wall ready to go? How cool is that?"

"Brilliant," said Rachel. "And I forgive you for calling the baby Fatso."

CHAPTER 18

LONDON, UK, SUNDAY

"How about we pack up a sandwich and a piece of fruit each, head off to the station, and make a day of Hyde Park?" Rebecca suggested to Sylvia following Sunday morning's breakfast of fruit toast and tea. "The weather is ideal, the exercise will be welcome, and there will be no one interrupting our quality time." Sylvia thought it a great idea, and to this end, ten thirty saw them sharing a park bench. Each nursed a takeaway coffee from a mobile vendor.

"It is lovely to get out of the house for a while. Regain perspective." Rebecca sipped her coffee.

"Yes. A perspective that includes watching horse riding lessons while we sip our coffee. All very tally-ho!" Sylvia took in the magnificence of the two stallions. "I'd go for the sleek black one—how about you?"

"The horse or the rider?" Rebecca enquired, grinning cheekily. They both laughed.

"I'd forgotten how funny you can be." Sylvia's smile faded. "Mum, I'm sorry about yesterday's outburst," Sylvia shifted her shoulder bag from her arm to beside her on the bench. "It was unfair of me."

"No. Not at all unfair. I don't know that I can ever fully explain … if you can ever fully understand. But we should both try, perhaps?" Rebecca took a few more sips of coffee. Her gaze followed the steady pace of the horses.

"The thing is, I loved, still love, your father. For me, there could never be anyone else. I took what I could get, as meagre as it was, although I didn't consider it meagre at the time. When your dad was with us, he was the kindest, most generous man. And he adored you. He still does. I just considered the way he behaved to be unconventional. Rather romantic. He was a sort of gallant knight in my eyes. I'm truly sorry for causing you pain. But not seeing him at all would have been worse, right?"

"I don't know. Part of me, a big part of me, thinks of him as a selfish bastard. I mean, why the hell couldn't he be here? Why couldn't we be enough for him?" Sylvia finished her coffee and crushed the cup. "But then, when he does deign to turn up, like the other night, I find myself feeling so bloody grateful." She located a mint from her bag. "He should be the one feeling grateful. Grateful that we can be bothered giving him the time of day. He even stays the bloody night! Sorry, but how can you do that?" Sylvia stood, took her coffee cup to a waste bin, and threw it in. Walking back to the bench, she put her shoulder bag over her arm once again. "We'd better make tracks if we're going to do any walking."

"Changing the subject ...," Rebecca said after they had walked silently for a few moments. "There is no point in Megan pursuing the poor vicar, is there? He appears to have everything in writing—a formal request, so to speak."

"It would seem so." Sylvia was pleased to talk about something else. "If I'm honest, I thought it was all quite marvellous. It was what Joe wanted. Nobody suffered in any way, for goodness' sake. So what if Megan was a little embarrassed? That's her problem. Bibi was surprised, yes, but not horrified. Viv and Tom were okay with it all, so ..." She found herself thinking of Tom momentarily. He had revealed another side of himself since she had arrived. More often than not off with his friends during their childhood, Sylvia and Viv were left to do their own thing. As an adult, he had seemed a little aloof. He was rather bookish and boring, but maybe he was merely thoughtful.

"So," Rebecca continued on her behalf, "Megan can stick it in her pipe and smoke it."

"Exactly!" said Sylvia, laughing heartily. "Take it or leave it."

"Like it or lump it."

"Put up or shut up."

"Okay. You win," Rebecca added, screwing up her cup and casting it into the recyclable bin. Shall we follow the horses?"

"I think you made a good point, earlier. Let's follow the sleek black one, shall we?"

PERTH, WEST AUSTRALIA, SUNDAY

"I am very concerned about Crystal, William." Brenda had sent Crystal on a minor errand that should take no longer than an hour.

"Are you?" William was feeling a little edgy after consuming his usual Sunday lunch prepared for him by Brenda. "I'm sure there's no need."

Drying the dishes as Brenda washed them, he had been a little surprised at the lack of comment on Crystal's improved attitude. He was quite ticked off and was taking great care not to clatter any of the dishes in case Brenda should sense any annoyance on his part. More often than not, Brenda would supply him with a foil container of leftovers, and the afternoon teas she conjured up for his luxury car clients were superb, especially considering the cut-price recompense he paid her. Of course, William had attributed Crystal's improved work ethic to himself rather than Ruth—or, indeed, Crystal herself.

"She's got this idea in her head that she wants to go to college to do a design course, whatever that is. "Sounds very airy-fairy to me. She needs to earn a living. These costumes she's making for—oh, I can't remember who or what. Well, you can't make a living out of that type of thing, can you? I think she said they were African, or Egyptian, or some such. On the other hand, everyone has to have a piece of paper nowadays. She can apply for college, but I don't see her getting a place."

William busied himself with neatening up the crockery cupboard to make a little more room. "Yes, Egyptian. They're for a theatrical performance. It's quite a lucrative commission." William stopped speaking abruptly. "I think these heyday cups and saucers are quite lovely, Brenda. You take such good care of them."

"Is it?" Brenda was washing the last of the cutlery. "Lucrative?"

William could have kicked himself for being caught off guard. "Well, relatively speaking, I was thinking of giving Crystal a small bonus on completion by way of encouragement. Delightful," he said as he picked up the last cup to be dried.

"But do you see her getting a place? Her school marks weren't much to boast about, were they? William, you know lots of people. Can't you pull a few strings … call in a few favours? She's just had too many rejections in her life; you know that. Her dad walked out. Mum brought her here. Her mum walked out. She didn't make friends at school. If I ban her from applying, she'll blame me for holding her back. If she applies and doesn't get in, it's another disappointment. I need your help here, William."

There were occasions when Brenda left one in no doubt as to expectations. Comply or she would make life uncomfortable. She knew William's history. In his younger days, before gaining his inheritance, William had a few wild years. There had been a spell in a detention centre. Brenda managed to secure him a job in a clothing factory, courtesy of one of her many relations, on the strict understanding that he would get his act together. To his credit, he didn't look back. His success was truly down to her. He had no idea, however, how he could exert any pressure or hold any influence over the prospective college intake.

William deliberately changed the subject. "Oh, Brenda, you remember that limo booking we discussed? Geoffrey is implying that it involves a very distinguished couple, Australian, but nonetheless … I can't ask outright, of course. We must keep it under wraps. They want the afternoon picnic and then wish to retain the car for the evening. They are bringing their own driver! Fancy that! It's not what I'd normally do, as you know. I shall charge extra. I'm wondering if it could be Hugh and Deborah. Or Nicole and Keith. Cate and …

what's-his-name. I'm sure I'll know when I see them to hand over the keys at the airport. Anyway, make it a bountiful picnic for three. Cloth napkins, the works."

Ben played golf with his father-in-law, Frank, regularly on a Sunday. He didn't mind golf. He had become reasonably adept at it over the years, and it was a pleasant way of keeping in with Frank and his group of well-heeled friends. Ben knew that Frank admired his business acumen. It was his financial success that had resulted in Frank and Gina's approval of him as a prospective son-in-law. It was true that Gina had harboured visions of higher social standing than that of a car salesman. But Suzanne was delighted. Frank felt sure that Ben had what it took to be successful. Frank had connections. He could put business his way. Suzanne would be kept in the manner to which Frank and Gina felt she deserved.

Today there were four of them. One of Frank's business associates had brought along his new young wife and was concentrating most of his effort on developing her swing (from behind, naturally), leaving Ben and Frank with frequent opportunities to talk amongst themselves.

"Business is continuing to boom, I trust?" Frank was selecting a suitable driver for a long hole. "Enrique was singing your praises to me earlier in the week."

"Ah, Señor Castro. Yes, a great deal for us. I wish he didn't have the name of a dictator, though. He sounds like a mobster when he opens his mouth, and he dresses like Robert De Niro."

"Nothing wrong with his money, Ben. That's what matters. So business is good, then. How's your health? Getting regular check-ups?" He set the ball on the tee and adjusted his stance.

"Check-ups?" Ben selected a driver for his forthcoming shot. "Not really. I think my health is pretty good."

"Best keep an eye on it, you know. Gina mentioned that Suzanne wasn't quite herself. She seemed a bit stressed. A bit worried. Gina thinks she might be a little unhappy for some reason. Frank practised his swing before taking his shot. "Ben, I don't have to remind you how important it is for you to ensure that Suzanne has no reason to feel anything other than contented. Gina and I rely on you to …" He took the swing. The ball flew through the air and landed in the middle of the fairway.

"Great shot," Ben commented.

"We rely on you to do the right thing. You do understand that, don't you?"

"Of course." Ben placed his ball on the tee. "Goes without saying, Frank." He hurried his shot, and it landed in the rough.

"Bad luck," said Frank, striding ahead.

"Shit," Ben muttered. He didn't need to be on the wrong side of Frank and Gina. They could make life very uncomfortable.

CHAPTER 19

PERTH, WESTERN AUSTRALIA, MONDAY

As usual, Alan checked his inbox upon arriving at the office. There were seven new messages. Two were from satisfied customers. Delvine would file those efficiently in the feedback log and add them to the website. One was an enquiry as to the availability of a particular vehicle. Robert would contact the customer promptly, assuring them that their purchase requirements would not be a problem. Three were selling products related to car maintenance or unique insurance deals, and one was from Nina. He read, "Thank you for ..." Alan presumed it would continue regarding the flowers. He would have to click on it to reveal the complete message. There was no way of knowing its content otherwise. His heart began beating at what he felt was twice its usual rate. He clicked on the box.

Thank you for the flowers. They were lovely.

Nina X

That was it. Alan didn't know what to think. Did she want to talk to him or not? Did she want to see him or not? The message was just over an hour old. She was probably at work. If he replied now, there was a chance she would see it almost immediately. But if he did respond straight away, what would she think? God. He had to reply, say something.

> Dear Nina,
>
> I'm so glad you liked the flowers. [scrub the "Dear."] Are gerberas still your favourites?
> Did you want to meet? [scrub the "meet" bit.]
>
> Alan X

She could reply or not reply. Please let her reply. Alan hit SEND.

"Mr. Meadows, we're almost out of coffee supplies. Shall I get some?"

"Yes, Delvine, thank you. All the receipts, please. And, Delvine, what about a vase of flowers in the coffee corner? Nice bright ones—like gerberas, for example. What do you think?"

"Flowers? Oh. They do nice bunches of flowers at the supermarket. I'm afraid I don't know much about flowers, apart from the obvious ones, like roses and daffodils. Will they last for very long in here? Would it be better to get a couple of plants?"

"Oh, I don't know. Perhaps you're right. Don't worry. It was just an idea. Robert, don't leave it too long before you follow through with that Volvo enquiry."

"I'm on it, boss," Robert said from behind the computer screen. "Just checking a few details."

Ben had arranged for both Mr. Forsythe's and Suzanne's cars to be fixed by Neville's mob over Sunday, Monday, and Tuesday. Neville liked having plenty of jobs on the go to keep everyone busy. George Forsythe didn't need a replacement vehicle for the few days his son's car

110

was out of action, as he and his wife had the grandchildren to stay over for a few days while their son was working away. They could efficiently manage the school runs with her car. Suzanne did need a replacement car, however, a small Honda. It wasn't flash, but it was in good repair.

It being a Monday, Suzanne dealt with all the laundry tasks, including fixing the dress that Pearl had damaged in her fight with Opal. It was the dress that she had worn for Pearl's christening—a well-cut white knee-length shift, designed to be worn beneath a yellow and white lace jacket. Opal would wear it over a white leotard and white leggings and present her haiku poem, "White," looking charming. It had mostly been ripped at the seam and wasn't challenging to mend.

Suzanne felt more in control. Before tackling the laundry, she had sorted out all the bank accounts using the regular fortnightly funds. At Ben's insistence, the money forfeited by Pearl was in a jar on a kitchen shelf. She had not put any money in her clothing account and intended to feed the family for two weeks on food that was already in the pantry, freezer, and refrigerator. Easy.

The diary had no entry over the weekend. Suzanne didn't want to risk its discovery. Retrieving it from its hiding place, she turned over the page bearing the self-hate message. If she could get through this fortnight, she'd be okay. That page would serve as a reminder. No more gambling. Double blank pages stared back at her. "Today I did the laundry," she scrawled at the top. She changed the word *laundry* into clothing items blowing in the breeze on a washing line. Slowly the whole page became covered in images of piles of family washing, boxes of laundry powder and pegs. Taps, sinks, suds. Bedding and towels cascaded from an open front loader. Socks and underwear spilt out of a plastic laundry basket. In the centre of the drawing, Suzanne had sketched a care instruction tag. It read, "Hand-wash separately."

Crystal had been thrilled with the progress of the Egyptian costumes. Geoffrey and Martin would be expecting a fitting soon. Geoffrey was always particularly encouraging. Ruth had kept her word, and they had shared out the small jobs equally. In return for Crystal's compliance without complaint, she had allowed Crystal to do most of the work relating to the costume order, as long as she referred to Ruth if she was not sure about anything or got into difficulty, rather than use guesswork and spoil or waste the fabric. The bright pink gum no longer made appearances.

Monday mornings were often quite slow. William had gone off on his usual "tour," as Ruth secretly referred to his regular check-ups on his various business interests. She was a little peeved, if she were to be honest with herself. Although grateful for a couple of weeks of unexpected employment given to her by William, she felt hurt that he had not acknowledged any improvement in Crystal's attitude and work ethic at all—either to her or Crystal. He kept banging on about the "celebrity" status interest being shown in his car hire efforts, courtesy of Geoffrey, even though he never actually recognised anyone famous. Geoffrey was probably stringing him along, knowing what a sucker he was for anything prestigious. Ruth knew that Brenda catered admirably for the afternoon teas and picnics. Somehow, William always seemed to gain from other people's hard graft. It wouldn't hurt him to try to call in a favour and get Crystal a place in a college somewhere. He knew a good many people.

Ruth asked Crystal to clear out each of the storage compartments, clean them thoroughly, and replace the contents tidily.

"There are scraps of material everywhere," Crystal remarked. "Odd shapes and odd sizes. Not large enough to do anything with on their own, but I reckon they could be worked together and made into cushion covers or bags."

"Possibly."

"Could I try, then?"

"Well, let's not get too carried away. If no other orders are waiting and the costume is completely ready for a fitting, then you can do me one. One cushion cover. But not at the expense of anything else, okay?"

"Wicked. I'll sort the scraps into colours."

Ruth accessed the numbers of two customers whose orders were ready for pick up, so she might advise them via text message.

A customer approached the counter and placed a school uniform blazer on the bench. Crystal left the material scraps and turned her attention to the customer. "What may I do for you?" she asked.

Jade had said very little about the auditions. Monday lunchtime would see the list of successful chorus cast members posted on the notice board. She knew she had auditioned well, but so had lots of others. Jade attended a dance school run by a talented young woman called Rosalie Jenkins. Rosalie was halfway through a six-month break after giving birth. Jade didn't want to go to an alternate class, opting instead to go with the break and then restart after Christmas. Privately, Suzanne had reasoned that Ben would be more inclined to say yes to the pony club—and of course a pony—if Jade no longer appeared to be doing dance classes. Surely there was a significant social advantage in riding rather than dancing.

Jade didn't quite know how this whole pony club thing had come about. Admittedly, the cute toys she collected when she was younger were cool, but she had never harboured any great desire to be an equestrian. Once the audition process started, Jade realised afresh how dancing made her soul soar. If she got a place in the chorus, she could even ask about private lessons. Riding lessons and ponies would cost more than dance lessons, wouldn't they? She could be honest about not wanting to have much at all to do with horses. Sophie was nice. But couldn't they enjoy doing different things and remain friends?

At the sound of the siren signalling the end of human biology, Jade gathered her stuff together at breakneck speed and made for the gym. She was the first one to reach the notice board. However, within a short space of time, students were jostling to read the list. Other students had pushed in front of her. She had to stand on tiptoe and peer between bobbing heads. She started reading from the top. Oh, they were listed alphabetically by surname. Meadows, Jade. "Meadows,

Jade!" she screamed, and then she covered her mouth. She could hardly breathe. She sank to the floor. Tears were running down her cheeks. She wanted this more than anything in the world. Her stomach was turning somersaults. In her excitement, Jade failed to notice a paragraph beneath the name list detailing some provisional details. She desperately wanted to share this with someone. Maybe she would try to find Chaplain Rachel.

CHAPTER 20

Jade could hardly wait to tell Suzanne about the successful audition. She heard Opal and Pearl squabbling before she saw them.

"It's not yellow; it's orange!" Pearl was yelling at Opal.

"No, it's not. It's more like yellow, isn't it, Mum?"

"What's yellow?" Suzanne was hurrying to keep up with them.

"The car we're using cos Jade broke the other one."

"She didn't break it! She smashed it! Didn't you, Jade? You smashed the car. See?" Opal was triumphant. "It's more like orange."

"It was an accident, so shut up about it. Who cares what colour the car is? Mum, guess what." Jade was jigging up and down with excitement.

"Mum, Jade said shut up to me. Mum!"

"I didn't say shut up to you. I said shut up about the car—that's different." Jade stopped jigging. "Mum, listen," Jade implored.

"Just a minute, Jade, please. *Girls,* get into the car and stop fighting. Dad has told me that there is to be no TV or computer time if you fight. The car is a cross between yellow and orange, and it doesn't matter anyway. Now, Jade wants to talk to me, so be quiet."

Jade thought her mother looked and sounded better than she had for a while. And she'd told her sisters to be quiet. "Mum, I passed the audition for the musical. I'm so happy!"

"Oh, fantastic." Suzanne had forgotten about the auditions; she was genuinely pleased. "What about Sophie?"

"Sophie didn't try out. Mum, I like Sophie. She's nice, but I don't like horses much."

"What do you mean? You love horses!"

"I don't. Not really. I want to be a dancer—a proper one. Could I have private lessons?"

Rachel tossed the salad with balsamic vinegar and placed the bowl on the table. Matt was trimming the fat from some steak. His shifts didn't allow him to have dinner at home with Rachel every day. They valued those occasions when they could talk about their day over dinner.

"It's so good to see the excitement generated by the musical. I'm quite jealous! I would have loved to have been given that opportunity in high school."

"Me too!" said Matt. He struck a pose: feet apart, arms outstretched to an imaginary audience. "Dum, dum, dum, de diddy, he sang as he mimicked slicking back a quiff of Travolta-styled greased hair. "I've got chills! They're multiplyin', and I'm loooosin' control!"

Rachel laughed. She placed her hands on her lower hips and swung them in time.

"You're the one that I want," she pouted provocatively, leaning forward and shimmying her shoulders. "Ow." She grabbed hold of the back of the chair. "Ow!" Pulling the chair out from beneath the table, Rachel sat down awkwardly. "Ow!" she said again.

Matt was beside her immediately. "What's the matter, Rachel? What's wrong?" He put his arms around her protectively. Breathe, darling. Breathe slowly and deeply."

The front door opened. Dee came through. "What's wrong, guys?" She was alarmed to see Rachel taking controlled breaths, with Matt leaning over her.

"Nothing. I think I'm fine. I just shouldn't be singing and dancing at the moment."

"You go and lie down for fifteen minutes while I do the barbecue, please. Dee, will you go with her to make sure she stays put for a little while?"

Geoffrey and Martin arrived together at Hutton's to collect and pay for their costumes.

"I insist you try them on one last time," William fawned, aware that he would be charging over the odds but was pretty sure he would get away with it.

"I don't know if we'll both fit around there!" Martin was excited. He did so love to dress up.

"Sure we shall." Geoffrey went ahead of him. Neither of us needs to be shy, now do we?" They both went into the changing booth and drew the curtain across.

William told Ruth and Crystal they could both stop for the day. In truth, he didn't want them to know how much he was charging for the costumes. Martin and Geoffrey emerged looking resplendent in white and gold. William was about to begin gushing with praise when he became aware of two police officers approaching the counter.

"Mr. Hutton?" one of them inquired.

"Yes. Is something wrong, Officer?"

"PC Dave Livingstone. He displayed his badge and indicated to his fellow officer. "PC Georgia Welles. Are you the owner of a black Holden Calais, registration SCV 947?"

William went cold. "I am, Officer. What's happened?"

"Your car has been found, presumed abandoned, in the staff-only section of the car park of the Perth Central Library, sir."

"What? Found in the … where?"

"The staff only section of the Perth Central Library car park."

"What the hell? Is it damaged?"

"It would appear not, sir. But it does need to be collected. It can't stay there. The library staff reported it rather than just having it towed away. Very considerate, actually."

"My God!" said Geoffrey. "That's one of the strangest things! Was there no immobiliser, then, William?"

"No. It's *a classic*. I'm retaining authenticity. However, maybe it wasn't the wisest move."

"We're all wiser in hindsight, aren't we, William?" Geoffrey oozed. "You'd better go and collect it, don't you think?"

William was stunned. "Yes, I had. But … erm …"

"Oh, you need someone to mind the shop? Literally." He smiled at the officers. "We could help out there, couldn't we, Martin?"

"No problem. We need a moment to change!"

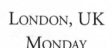

LONDON, UK
MONDAY

Sylvia found herself at a bit of a loose end on Monday. Rebecca had to return to work. Vivienne had to attend to some business. Bibi wanted to spend most of the day replying to condolence emails. There were messages from those unable to participate in the funeral and several from friends and acquaintances she had not seen for some time. Also, in the afternoon, Bibi had a home appointment with the family solicitor to ensure all was as it should be. The lounge room of the big house featured a wall lined with bookcases stashed with a diverse collection of books in varying states of repair, as well as volumes by contemporary authors. There were dated videotapes, sets of CDs and DVDs, boxes of keepsakes and photographs, and half-filled albums. Bibi had suggested that she might enjoy spending a few hours perusing what was there. Sylvia was smiling at a photo of herself and Vivienne dressed in hula skirts. Her mobile rang.

"Tom!" she answered.

"Hi, Sylvia. Are you out with Vivi, today?"

"No. Unexpected business meetings. I'm just amusing myself with a bit of time travel. In other words, I'm looking at old photos. Why?"

"Well, you can say no, of course, but I've brokered a deal with my fellow lecturer. She's going to combine her tutorial time with my scheduled session this afternoon. I'm going to do the same for her next week. So that leaves me free from midday onwards. I thought maybe a spot of lunch and then the Tate Modern."

"Oh, Tom, that sounds wonderful. Are you sure? I don't want to feel guilty about taking you away from hard-working fee-paying students!"

"Don't worry. I put way more time in than strictly required. So is that a yes, then?"

"What about Bibi? She'll be on her own."

"Ah. What time are you expecting Viv back?"

"She just said after lunch. Bibi's got an appointment here with the solicitor at one."

"I'll phone back in five."

Tom was back on the phone within a few minutes. Viv was due back at about two o'clock. Perhaps Sylvia could make a sandwich for Bibi and leave the house at about twelve. Tom was sure that Bibi wouldn't mind. Sylvia needed to catch the train from Peckham to Blackfriars. There was a neat little cafe called Triffids, and it was close to the station. Could they meet there?

Sylvia checked the arrangements with Bibi, who seemed more than happy with everything. No longer in need of the wheelchair in the house, Bibi felt sure she could manage for about an hour. Once the solicitor had left and Vivienne had arrived, she might have a bit of a lie-down.

"I think I recognise that raincoat, don't I?" Tom stood as Sylvia came through the door of the cafe.

"I'm sure you do. I've been grateful for the key to the spare wardrobe afforded me by Vivienne. I love that mural." Sylvia was admiring the scene painted over an entire wall, depicting the classic post-apocalyptic novel *Day of the Triffids*.

"Great, isn't it? Odd for a cafe, I suppose, but somehow it works. The proprietor is a big John Wyndham fan.

Sylvia peeled off her black gloves and unwound the scarf from her neck." I managed to squeeze these into my suitcase, thank goodness. I don't need them now, to be honest. But when we leave the gallery later, I'll be glad of them. What do you recommend?" Sylvia picked up the menu and perused it.

"The chicken, bacon, and brie focaccias are good, but have whatever you fancy." Tom didn't pick up a menu. He had made his own choice. Tom placed an order. Sylvia observed his manner. He was pleasantly and quietly confident, she decided, comfortable in his skin. Despite being the brother of her best friend, she knew very little about him. What was it with her whole upbringing that seemed to keep everybody distant?

When Tom returned from the counter, she was locating her Oyster card. "I suddenly remembered that after I swiped my card, I placed it in my bag rather than my wallet. I wouldn't want to lose it!"

"Cripes, no! I reckon people have committed murdered for an Oyster! I think it's a political conspiracy to keep us all submissive. "Whatever you say, Officer. Just please let me keep my Oyster card!"

It was late afternoon when Sylvia and Tom emerged from the gallery.

"Thank you, Tom. I appreciate your giving me time. I think I'd forgotten how much of a Londoner I am." She pulled on her gloves. "Australia is very different. I love Perth. The climate is wonderful. The beaches are glorious, the people friendly and open, but ..."

"You miss the cold and the rain. The smog and the grime. The crowds and the traffic. I understand completely!"

He picked up her hand and linked her arm through his. "I feel responsible for your safety. Rush hour and all."

"Do you think the colour red is particularly significant? In London, I mean. The buses are red. There are still phone boxes, and they are red. The underground signs ..."

"They stand out, I suppose. I've had several holidays abroad and a few lecture tours. Although I haven't lived anywhere else, I'm always happy to come back to London. It's steeped in history, and it sort of—I don't know—encapsulates a grandeur that belongs to everyone. Not all the population would agree with me, of course. There are plenty who long to tear it all down." Tom stopped deliberately at the kerb and pressed the button for the crosswalk. "You mentioned people, Sylvia. Is there a particularly special person?" Tom kept her arm linked in his but shoved his hands into his pockets. The walk sign lit up. They walked across the street towards the station; Tom checked his watch. "Hey. If we hurry, we'll catch the five fifteen."

His question had remained unanswered.

CHAPTER 21

PERTH, WESTERN AUSTRALIA, TUESDAY

William absented himself from the mall for several hours on Tuesday. He painstakingly cleaned his precious car himself, inside and out. He scrubbed, vacuumed, polished, and buffed until it gleamed once more. He felt outraged. Taking his woes to Brenda, he sat in her kitchen while she baked and cooked. He drank her tea and ate her home-baked cake. She was sympathetic, it was true, but her mind was on something else, he thought. And she commented more than once that it could have been worse. Well, he knew that. But it was still genuinely dreadful. He hoped to receive a container of spaghetti Bolognese for that night's dinner. He hoped in vain.

"I must get back to the mall. Goodness, that Bolognese smells delicious, Brenda."

"Yes. You probably need to get back, William. Life goes on."

"William, you poor love. We all know how prized that car is to you. Did you pick it up without too much hassle? Was there any damage?"

William was pleased to hear Ruth expressing a higher level of concern. "Ruth, I have to tell you that this has all been very disturbing. Very stressful." Ruth nodded sympathetically. "The car wasn't damaged, but it had been driven around a fair bit, obviously, because there was hardly any fuel in it at all. And whoever took it had been eating pizzas. There were boxes and crumbs everywhere. No respect. The police wouldn't dust it for fingerprints! Can you believe that? They told me human resources couldn't be justified because no one was injured and the car wasn't damaged. Justify human resources! I said to them, 'That's why these things happen—because they get away with it.'" William sat down heavily in one of the chairs. "And there was mud."

"Mud?" queried Ruth.

"In the back. Some great oaf with size ten boots, I'd say, had been stomping mud in the back. Dreadful."

"Oh dear," said Ruth. "As you say, William, no respect."

"None at all, Ruth. None at all."

Ruth felt that William was close to tears. "Still, I suppose it could have been worse."

William glared. "Well, yes. There were no cigarette butts," he commented with the utmost seriousness.

"Can I get you a cup of tea?" Ruth offered.

"I'll put the kettle on," Crystal said hurriedly. "Ruth brought in some Earl Grey."

"Thank you kindly." William was soaking up empathy. "I shall have a cup of tea, and then I shall check on the dry-cleaners. I was so upset about the recent turn of events that I didn't check in last evening or this morning. I don't need to, though. They're reliable."

Reliable and cheap, William reminded himself.

Alan was trying not to check his email every five minutes. He had to wait for Nina to reply. But for how long? Was it just a matter of "Thanks for the nice flowers," with no more to be said? He hadn't fallen in a hole. Not yet.

Sylvia was due home in a couple of days. Sylvia. He'd hardly given her a thought, if he was being honest. They had agreed that it would be best not to worry about sending each other messages and phoning.

There was a time difference, for one thing. But more importantly, Alan felt that Sylvia needed unencumbered time with the people she would be visiting in London. And all of them were grieving.

What was he to do, though, if Nina did say she wanted to meet, that there was a real possibility she could come back into his life? Was he kidding himself, anyway? Why did she leave in the first place? Why did she hurt him so badly? Had she found someone else? God. Why was it so complicated and fraught with problems?

"Hey, boss. Should I take this customer? Or would you prefer to?"

"Yes. Sorry, Robert. I was checking something over." Alan quickly walked out into the car yard. Did he see Robert and Delvine exchange curious looks? Having determined to get a grip, he spent almost an hour with the customer and almost forgot to offer the upgraded car detail for the newly purchased vehicle as part of the deal.

Alan's heart skipped a beat when he saw a reply from Nina—with an attachment! He accessed it immediately.

"Yes, gerberas are still my favourite." Alan clicked on the attachment. It was a photo of a multitude of brightly coloured gerberas.

"I've missed you," Alan wrote. SEND.

Alan was surprised to see Suzanne drive into the yard a short while later. Neville had been checking over the trade-in vehicles and was advising Alan as to the availability of suitable cars. "The latest five are good to go, but the Datsun is a let-down. Needs to go to scrap."

"No worries, Nev. I thought the Datsun was touch-and-go."

"Hello, Neville. Hello, Alan." Suzanne alighted from the loaned Honda.

"Well, hello, Mrs. Meadows. What an unexpected pleasure. You look very nice."

"Thank you, Neville. I have a full day today, Alan. I'm just wondering if my car is fixed and ready to go. I don't much like driving the Honda. I don't feel confident in it, you know. Silly, isn't it?"

"Actually, it's ready. I'll get one of the boys to drive it around, and you can take it if you like." Neville moved away from them and put a call through to the workshop. Suzanne was a good-looking woman, no doubt about that. But for Nev, most people fell into one of two categories. People were either sinkers or swimmers. It didn't have much to do with money or background. His mother, Aileen, ran a tight ship and had made their business successful. It wasn't flashy, but they made a more than decent living and had an excellent reputation. His father, Raymond, was well respected amongst black and white fellas. No mean achievement. However, in truth, although Raymond had the impression that he had made his way through his determination, it was Aileen who had been in charge and made everything work. He reckoned that Ben's wife, Suzanne, didn't swim too well. Moreover, she didn't know where the life jackets were.

Alan had also noticed that Suzanne appeared immaculate as usual, but she seemed distracted and slightly nervous for some reason. They watched her drive off in her familiar car.

"By the way, boss, what we doin' with the camper van? It can't stay here much longer. It takes up room and looks out of place. One of the guys can take it to Camp Right—no worries.

"No." Alan felt panic rise in his chest. He couldn't let it go, not yet. Somehow, it was tied up with his regaining Nina. Of course, he couldn't tell anyone about it. They would think he was mad. Perhaps he was mad. "I thought Schubert was using it to visit his mob."

"He brought it back this morning. So that older couple didn't want it?

"Erm, no. Well, I haven't been given a definite answer, to be honest with you. You're right. It can't stay there. Just two more days, please, Nev? Then I'll let you know one way or the other."

"Whatever you say, boss." Neville hung up the phone and took a rather derisory look over at the camper van. What was the boss thinking?

Alan was relieved. He had to get in contact with Nina. Sylvia was due back on Friday. God, what was he going to do? Should he say, "Hi, Sylvia! Welcome home. Have a good trip? How was the funeral? Just ignore the camper van and I'll put the kettle on. Oh, this is about Nina, by the way. She's come back into my life now. She's quite happy to sleep in the camper van until we get sorted. There's no rush for you to move out. I mean, take your time ..."

God. Really. What was he going to do?

The task of issuing permission slips from the office and answering any student questions fell to Rachel. She drew each student's attention to the clause regarding costumes. They were to be responsible for providing their costume requirements, subject to approval by the wardrobe department. They also had to contribute two payments of eighty dollars, due a fortnight apart, to assist with the cost of engaging a "professional" choreographer/dance instructor (care of the university drama department's graduating year).

There had been a rush of successful students handing in forms. Rachel had ticked off all the names, except for two. Peter Ramble's mother had phoned to say he had to attend a doctor's appointment and would be in later that morning. Jade Meadows was the other. A little odd, Rachel thought, seeing as she knew how excited Jade would have been to have gotten through the audition. Maybe she would put a call through to her mother. Erin Waterford was there in tears because her name wasn't on the list. Rachel was patiently explaining that there were several who didn't make it. There was a substitute list they could add their name to in case of any casting mishaps. But the most positive thing to do was to get involved with the backstage crew and try again next year.

"Mrs. Meadows?" Rachel had waited until after morning tea break to see if Jade's form came in. She wouldn't usually play catch-up on behalf of students; they needed to be responsible, but she was a little concerned, as Jade had seemed upset. Something could be wrong.

"Yes. Suzanne speaking."

"Suzanne, Rachel Kirk here."

"Oh, hello. Has something happened?"

"No, nothing's wrong. I just wanted to check with you that Jade would be returning her permission slip regarding participation in the musical. Signatures are crucial. Sooner rather than later!"

"Oh. Of course. I'm afraid I haven't seen a form. Jade must have forgotten to show it to me in her excitement."

"Well, that's okay. If you call in this afternoon, we can do it then. I have additional forms. You are aware that the students supply their costumes, subject to the approval of the wardrobe department?"

"Oh, okay." Suzanne thought it was far from okay, as she hadn't done any real needlework for years.

"And there are the two eighty-dollar payments that have to be made to the drama department to cover the cost of choreography."

Suzanne felt her legs go weak.

CHAPTER 22

The only way visitors could access high school premises was through the main office door.

"Good afternoon." Suzanne was pleased she had dressed carefully. It boosted her confidence. "Might I be able to speak to the school chaplain?"

"Mrs. Meadows, isn't it? For Jade?"

"Yes. I wanted to see the chaplain regarding Jade. Would that be possible?"

"Let me see if she's available." The receptionist picked up the phone and accessed Rachel's extension. "She would be happy to see you now, if you like."

"Thank you. Where …?" This was perfect. Hoping to see the chaplain rather than one of the office staff, Suzanne planned on relating a convincing story to explain why she couldn't make the first of the two eighty-dollar payments immediately. She hoped a chaplain might well be more accommodating.

Rachel was pleased to have the opportunity to speak to Mrs. Meadows informally. She might be able to discern if Jade had reason to be concerned. Rachel noticed the family resemblance straight away. "Come in, Mrs. Meadows. Take a seat."

"Suzanne, please. You kindly telephoned about Jade's form and the two eighty-dollar payments. Jade hasn't given me a form, I'm afraid. I shall need another. As for the first payment, I must apologise. It's the silliest thing, but I was at my mother's and she was asking me if I liked this particular bag. I was giving it a try-out, you know, seeing if everything fitted in the pockets and so on. She was filling me in on information about her best friend, who has just been through an operation, and I must have failed to transfer everything into my usual bag. My purse, my phone, and all my cards are at my mother's place. It's such a nuisance. I'd hate Jade to miss out because of my carelessness. May I bring in the money in a day or two?"

"I'm sure a day or two won't hurt. But there is a reserve list for places, you need to understand. It wouldn't be fair to allow too much time. I'll say Thursday, but I must check with the office staff. I'm merely the chaplain—no clout!" Rachel took in the way Suzanne looked. Terrific, actually. A bit showy, but you wouldn't consider her down on her luck. Not that looks ever told the full story, of course. The tale of woe seemed implausible. You'd go collect the purse or someone would drop it off to you surely? Perhaps Jade had discerned correctly, and there were money problems.

"Let's go down to the office now. You can fill in the form. I'll see if I can wield any influence to allow you a little extra time." On reaching the reception desk, Rachel experienced a crippling pain. She bent forward and grabbed hold of the desk. "Ow." She breathed deeply. The receptionist came around to the other side of the desk, very concerned. She led Rachel to a seat. Suzanne could see the forms on the desk. She quickly grabbed a form and a pen, printed Jade's name, signed it and ticked the box that read, "$160 paid in full." She placed it under the pile of similar notes.

"Oh my goodness." Suzanne came across to both women. Rachel had gone deathly white. "What's wrong?"

"Oh, oh," Rachel moaned.

"I'll phone for an ambulance. Don't worry. I'm sure you're fine. You're not quite due yet, are you?" The last thing the receptionist wanted was to assist at an unscheduled birth.

Rachel shook her head and grimaced.

"I'll take her to the hospital. It will be quicker. My car is right outside." Suzanne had been able to park in one of the few spots close to the office because there was half an hour to go before school was out for the day. "You'd rather go now, wouldn't you?" Suzanne looked at the staff name badge. "Rachel? Shall I take you in my car?"

"I think I should ring for an ambulance ..." The receptionist looked distinctly uneasy.

"But if we go now, we'll be at the hospital by the time the ambulance would have arrived. Rachel, do you want to come with me?"

"I don't know." Rachel breathed heavily and deliberately. "I don't want a fuss. Ooooh ..."

"If you check everything out at the hospital and they send you home, then there's no harm done, is there?" Suzanne encased Rachel's hands in her own. She recalled the trauma of birth very well.

"Okay." Rachel grimaced as she stood. "If you're sure you don't mind."

"We'll ring when we get to the hospital so you know all is well." While it was true that Suzanne was keen to be out of the way of the forms on the reception desk, she felt genuinely pleased with the opportunity to take control of the situation.

Helping Rachel into the car and heading off for the hospital, she experienced a sense of empowerment as she spoke calmly to Rachel about how soon she would be in the capable hands of nursing staff. They dealt with this kind of thing every day and knew what to do. When incriminating images of the permission slip came into her mind's eye, she swept them away. She'd get the money from either her mother or Ben and take it into school, where the "mistake" on the form could easily be explained away because of the trauma of the moment. Anyway, this was going to be the last time.

Opal was climbing on the play equipment not too far from Mrs. Bender's classroom. Pearl was searching for stray pieces of Sticky Tack adhering to the brick wall where the bags were stored. "Where's Mum?"

Pearl gave up on her not particularly fruitful search and ran across to join Opal. "I don't know, do I?"

"Oh, I want a juice box. Where is Mum?"

"I said I don't know, didn't I?" Opal stopped climbing and jumped down from the lower ladder into the sandpit beneath. Brushing off her legs, she looked around and realised they were alone. Mum was always on time.

Mrs. Bender appeared at the door. "Is your Mum not here, girls? That's unusual. She's probably held up in traffic or something. We'll wait five minutes and then I'll phone her."

Pearl started to wail. "I want a juice box. Where is she?"

"I've got a juice box," Mrs. Bender said, walking into her classroom and returning moments later with two drinks and a packet of biscuits, kept for occurrences such as this. Handing each of the girls a box and a cookie, she directed them to the bench. It was closer to ten minutes when Mrs. Bender phoned Suzanne. A pert voice advised that the call recipient was unavailable.

Mrs. Bender took another two biscuits out of the pack. "I'll put these away and then take you both up to the office. We'll soon find out what's going on. Mrs. Bender hated these instances. No one was happy until children and a responsible adult were united. It was very odd for Suzanne not to be there, and she had seemed troubled lately.

As soon as Pearl saw the office, she burst into tears. "I don't want to go in there without Mummy. I want Mummy!" Tears coursed down her face.

Mrs. Bender was both surprised and gratified to see Opal drop her bag and envelop Pearl in her arms. "Don't cry, Pearl. Mummy will be here soon. It's all right." Opal looked up at Mrs. Bender, who noticed tears brimming in her eyes also.

"Girls, we have to go into the office to check Mummy or Daddy's number. I'll wait with you."

Opal took Pearl's hand and led her through the door. "Come on, Pearl. Mrs. Bender will help us."

Swiftly paced footsteps gave way to running as Jade came around the corner of the office block and saw her two sisters. "Opal, Pearl, what's happened? Where's Mum?"

"Hello, Jade." Carol Bender remembered their older sister. "Mum seems to be running a little late, Jade. I'm about to check telephone numbers. Can I leave the girls to you for a few minutes?"

Pearl began a new torrent of tears and grasped Jade's legs, burying her face in Jade's skirt. "I want Mummy!" she sobbed.

"It's all right, Pearl. Let's sit over here. Look, here are some books."

Once again, Opal's teacher was pleased to see another side to all three girls. Typically she saw them fighting. Well, the younger two anyway. She quickly explained the problem and asked for confirmation of the phone number. It appeared to be correct, so she dialled again and got the same response. Ben had been the emergency contact number.

"Suzanne isn't there? I'm very sorry. I'll be with you as soon as I can. It's about a ten-minute drive."

"I can't apologise enough, Mrs. Bender." Ben was attempting to extricate himself from Pearl's vice-like grip. She had been the first to see Ben coming around the corner to the office and had burst her way out of the door towards him with a new rush of tears. Her two sisters and Carol Bender followed in a more sedate fashion; however, everybody seemed to be speaking at once.

"Where's Mum?" asked Jade.

"Why are you here instead of Mum?" demanded Opal.

"I want to go home!" yelled Pearl.

"I don't know where Mum is. I'd say it's either traffic or a bit of car trouble. Right now I'm going to take you home."

"Why won't she answer the phone?" Jade was angry. "For goodness' sake."

"Thank you again, Mrs. Bender. You have no idea, I suppose, where Suzanne is if she's not answering her phone?"

"No. I'm afraid not, Mr. Meadows. It's most unlike her to be late, but ..."

"Jade, would you take the girls over to the bench there and make sure they have everything in their bags, please. Homework and whatever." Ben indicated towards the bench and hoped Jade would pick up on the hint. She looked at Mrs. Bender, who mouthed a silent "Thank you" in her direction.

Once out of earshot, Carol Bender whispered, "I'm sure there's a simple explanation, but Suzanne has seemed a little, well, stressed lately."

"Stressed?" Ben questioned. "Stressed how?"

"Oh, I've no idea. I mean, we're all stressed, aren't we?" Carol laughed nervously. But you know, sometimes things get on top of us more than usual. Anyway, I'll let you get your girls home. I'm sure everything's fine. Thank you for coming so promptly."

CHAPTER 23

Suzanne drove around to the emergency department and parked while she accompanied Rachel into reception. Leaving her with medical staff, she moved her car to a more satisfactory parking bay and made her way back inside. Rachel had been allocated a bed while she waited to see a doctor. She looked calmer and was no longer in pain. Suzanne glanced up at the clock on the wall directly behind Rachel's bed. It was six minutes after four.

"Oh my God! It's after four o'clock! Whatever was I thinking! The girls. I'm so late. Oh my God!"

"Heavens!" Rachel's hand went to her mouth. "Oh, Mrs. Meadows, I'm so sorry. Leave now—go. The nurse has called Matthew. I feel terrible for making you so late. Go!"

"I can't even phone anyone," Suzanne said exasperatedly.

"I'll call the school and say you're on your way. Go. I'll get the number from one-two-three-four. Clearview Primary, right?"

Suzanne moved with as much speed as her heels would allow. Her phone was, in fact, in the boot of her car, along with the other items she claimed to have left at her mother's. She was almost running by now, and her mind was racing. The girls would be beside themselves. Hurtling through the automatic doors, she ran straight into a woman whose view was partially obscured by several bunches of flowers crammed into two

134

buckets she was clutching around her middle. Suzanne's heels gave way from beneath her. The buckets dropped to the ground. One remained upright, while the other toppled and spilt its contents all over Suzanne. The firmly packed floral arrangements remained relatively unscathed. However, the water content from the spilt bucket covered Suzanne's face, soaking half of her hair, and the bucket itself scraped its way over her left cheek, causing a livid-looking graze.

The two women were stunned. Three recovering patients sat helplessly on benches under the porch. One had the presence of mind to call out to two ambulance officers returning to their vehicle, who both rushed over to assist. Between them, they managed to set the two victims upright.

"Come and sit over here on this bench." One of the officers was holding on to Suzanne's arm, attempting to lead her in the direction of the seating.

"No, no. I'm in a terrible hurry. I'm so late for the school run. My daughters will be anxious and upset." Suzanne was hobbling.

The florist picked up a stray shoe, the loose heel of which languished sorrowfully. She handed the broken shoe to Suzanne. "Is your car close at hand? I mean, I can ..." Realisation slowly dawned. "Just a minute. Don't I know you?"

Suzanne looked more intently at her wrestling opponent and moved to relieve her of the damaged shoe. Sharp pain in her wrist made her squirm. "Ow. Look, I'm sorry. That was my fault. I'm in such a tearing hurry. Wait. Nina?"

"I don't believe it! Suzanne!"

"You need to get that wrist checked out," the second officer interjected testily, "and I can't leave an emergency vehicle over there. So I suggest you conduct your touching reunion in the admissions waiting room. You might not be able to drive."

Nina retrieved her phone from the pouch she wore around her waist. She checked the time: four fifteen. "There would be an emergency number for them to phone, wouldn't there? Your children might have already been picked up. Do you want to use my phone to check? Can you remember the number? If you know they're safe, you won't have to panic."

Suzanne went to take the phone and winced with pain.

"Tell me the number." On hearing the dial tone, Nina held the phone to Suzanne's ear without comment. Establishing that their father had collected all three girls, Suzanne relaxed a little. She cradled her wrist as it began throbbing. "Why don't we see if you can get that wrist strapped? I'll come with you. I just have to deliver these flowers to the gift shop. Very popular with visitors dropping in after work, you see."

As the accident had happened on hospital grounds, the staff proved diligent about offering first aid. However, Suzanne had to take her place in the queue after being assessed by the triage nurse. Nina suggested she stay with her in case she was unable to drive home.

"It must be painful for you. I think it's probably a strain. I'd be surprised if it's broken. We won't have to wait too long." Nina looked at the other two outpatients waiting for attention. One had a child with her who appeared to be having trouble remaining still. An elderly gentleman was breathing shallowly and closing his eyes periodically. Nina was pleased to see him stand when the nurse called. The nurse came across to assist in his attempts to go through to the doctor.

"It's bizarre seeing you like this." Suzanne didn't think she had broken her wrist either. Not enjoying the pain or the humiliation of looking such a complete mess, once she knew the girls were safe, she was glad to have somewhere to be other than home. "How long is it? You know, since you left? I mean, Alan was—well, we all were …"

"I know. I know. It's so hard to try to explain. It's been just over three years. Well, I've been back here for almost a year. I came back to try to put things right. No, that's not quite true."

"Cindy Jacobs?" The woman and child accompanied the nurse, leaving them alone.

"How are things with you? Apart from being an outpatient in A and E with a broken heel on a rather expensive pair of, what, Jimmy Choos? And if you don't mind my saying so, a potentially ruined outfit and hairdo. How's life?" Nina giggled.

Suzanne looked at Nina. She was seeing the woman she had known before, yet there was something different about her. Before leaving, Nina had rather shrivelled. Now she seemed far more together, even though she couldn't explain whatever it was that had caused her dramatic disappearance. It was refreshing to be with someone who wanted to talk to her about … well … her. She ran her fingers rather ineffectually through her drying hair. Stray pieces of flower stalks were caught up in it. "If I'm honest, Nina, not too well." She repeated the exercise with her hair, pulling out some of the debris. "Awful. Absolutely bloody fucking awful. I've—"

"Suzanne Meadows?" Suzanne winced as she got up from her chair.

It dawned on Nina that Suzanne had not once asked if she could borrow the mobile to call Ben.

The doctor approached Rachel's bedside at the same time as Matthew, who was relieved to see that both were smiling and relaxed.

"Geez, you scared me. Is everything okay?" Matthew went pale.

The doctor moved to his side quickly and guided him to a chair beside Rachel's bed. "Steady," she said. "Judging by the uniform, you're used to dealing with far more stressful situations than this!" She poured some water into a glass from a jug on the bedside table and handed it to him.

Matthew took a few gulps. "Thank you. Yes, yes, of course. I'm sorry."

"Your wife, your baby, right?" Matthew nodded. The colour began to return to his face. "I would say you are probably experiencing Braxton Hicks contractions, seeing as they have stopped while you have been resting."

"I've heard of those. Not the real thing. I feel a bit daft. Sorry, Matt." Rachel smiled reassuringly at Matthew.

"I'll do an examination and we'll see. Do you want to stay here or wait outside?"

Matthew took Rachel's hand. "I'll stay. I'm fine now."

The examination confirmed the doctor's opinion. "All pregnancies and births are different, but I think it's not going to be long before the baby is fully engaged. Are you prepared, just in case?"

"Yes, the room's ready. We weren't quite sure about dates at the beginning, were we, Matthew?"

"The room is ready. But I want you to have a rest from work. I'm ringing the school—no arguments."

Ben took the girls home. Opal and Pearl ran through the house, expecting to find Suzanne in there somewhere. When they discovered she was not there waiting for them, they both started to cry again.

"Where is she? Where's Mummy?" Both sisters sank to the floor and gave way to real tears. Ben was at a loss.

"We have sandwiches when we come home, usually peanut paste," said Jade. "Shall I make some?"

"I can do that. What about if you take the girls into the TV room and put something on to distract them?"

Jade nodded. Ben gave her a grateful hug and kissed the top of her head. "Thanks, sweetheart." Locating bread and peanut paste in the fridge, he set about his task without much enthusiasm. Where the hell was she? He was becoming seriously worried. He took the sandwiches and some milk to the girls. Jade had found a favourite movie and was sitting on the sofa with a younger sibling on either side. She gave each of them a sandwich and placed a cup of milk in front of them. They set about devouring the food hungrily and didn't seem to have the energy for fighting.

"There's a sandwich for us in the kitchen." Ben hoped Jade might be able to come up with a plausible explanation for her mother's absence. He realised he knew very little about what went on in the household on a day-to-day basis.

"Okay. I'll be back in a minute."

Ben walked back into the kitchen and accessed his mobile. He wondered if Suzanne might have contacted the school since he collected the girls. He was about to key in the number when Jade rejoined him.

"Dad, I know I shouldn't have done this. It's private, and I haven't looked inside—honest. But wouldn't it be okay for you to look?" She handed him Suzanne's diary.

CHAPTER 24

LONDON, UK, TUESDAY

"Thank you," Vivienne said as she moved the cup of tea closer. Sylvia had invited Viv and Bibi in for a chat. It was a rainy day, and they felt best served by staying indoors. "I'm sorry not to have been with you yesterday. Although from what I've heard, you were well entertained!" Vivi sipped her tea as she caught Sylvia's eye pointedly."

"Business to deal with, I understand." Sylvia picked up her cup, turning her attention to Bibi. "Our Viv is very high-powered, isn't she? We haven't done any of those things you researched for us so diligently, have we, Bibi? We've hardly any time left now."

"Oh, I've just enjoyed seeing you." Bibi took the biscuit from the plate. "I love shortbread."

"Were the business meetings worthwhile?" Sylvia so admired Vivienne. She made things happen.

"I am hoping so, although it may be a little soon to say more."

"Don't do that!" Sylvia put down her teacup and pushed it away. "You owe us!"

"Do I?" Vivi took several more sips of tea.

"No! But tell us what's going on anyway."

Vivienne dropped her voice playfully and adopted an Eastern European accent. "Can I trust you?"

"Vivienne! Spill the beans!"

Vivienne placed her teacup on the table with the others. "You remember Draper's Corner?"

"Oh, yes. That lovely square courtyard with small shops on three sides? In Southwark? Market stalls are crammed into the central yard created by the shops. The crowds give it a real buzz. I think each store has a stall, plus there are a few independents. The market operates on Friday, Saturday, and Sunday. Most of the shops are open every day except Monday. They have unusual clothing and accessories, plus bags and jewellery."

"You've got it. I'm interested in one that is becoming vacant." Viv relieved Bibi of her cup. "Refill?"

"No! Seriously? That's fantastic!" Except that it wasn't. Not really. It was for Vivienne, naturally. But she, Sylvia, was returning to what? Zips and pockets, as Crystal would say. Was she destined to stay in that uninspiring shopping mall until she retired? God. Living in Australia was meant to be an adventure. The job at Hutton's was to be temporary until an excellent opportunity presented itself. Yes, she had the market stall outlet for her work via Vivienne, but it was spasmodic at best.

Sylvia thought of Alan too. Where was the passion? The achievement? The goal setting? Where was the bloody living?

"Sorry. Back in a moment." Sylvia rushed from her seat to the bedroom and closed the door. She picked up the hem of her skirt and smothered her face with it. *Don't let them hear me. Please don't let them hear me,* she pleaded silently. Stuffing some of the material from the skirt into her mouth, she sobbed and sobbed.

Sylvia waited several minutes before emerging. Vivienne was drying the cups after washing them. She and Bibi were discussing the classic designs of the small eclectic crockery collection. "This is a lovely, restful room. Rebecca has good taste." They both looked up a little awkwardly at Sylvia.

"You all right?" Vivienne paired up the cups and saucers.

"I'm sorry." Sylvia picked up one cup and saucer carefully, as she was a little shaky.

"I'll do that," Vivienne took them from her. "We were just saying how lovely this room is."

"Yes. Yes, it is. Look, I'm sorry. I don't quite know what's gotten into me since I've been here. All this crying and carrying on … Honestly. It's pathetic."

"No, it isn't, Sylvia. Emotions are running high for all of us. You haven't seen your mum in ages. Your dad turns up out of the blue—big shock. Not helped by me, I must say. Plus the reason for us all being here. Joe was practically your grandfather too. Now you're about to head home. We've had very little time."

"Yes, of course. But I've embarrassed us all. I am sorry and shall try to act like a grown up! But I'm going to take a walk down to the corner shop. I was in there the other day, and I noticed a stand of travel aids. I'm going to get a travel pillow like yours."

Walking down to the store that was quite literally situated on the corners of Elizabeth and Charles Streets, Sylvia looked about her. Almost every house had a car parked in the street. Several had also concreted front yards to accommodate a vehicle. Although the solidly built houses had all been erected over a hundred years ago and had initially been occupied by residents of similar financial means, they were all a little different. Many had been chopped and changed, with bits added and bits removed. Some divided into the main house and a small flat. Boasting various states of repair or disrepair, Sylvia loved them. The corner shop she was about to patronise had very little room for cars. Most of its business was due to walk-by sales as well as local patronage. Mr. Rawipindu and his wife, Queenie, always seemed to be there, from early until late, serving any and every customer with a warm smile and a touch of small talk at no extra charge.

Returning to the flat, Sylvia owned her feelings of envy towards Vivienne. She was her best friend; there was no doubt about that. Viv had always been the powerhouse, though. Here she was about to open up a shop and market stall. Surrounded by the vibrancy of the colours and materials she worked with, Viv would be in her element. Sitting behind the sewing machine at Hutton's, Sylvia would be bored witless.

William's rather supercilious mannerisms invaded her headspace. Alan was still in love with his wife. Suddenly, she knew. She knew with absolute certainty that she didn't want to go back.

LONDON, UK, TUESDAY

Vivienne was packing. She heard the phone ring and waited to see if Bibi answered it, as she had left her in the sitting room with a magazine. Having grown adept at packing over recent years, she could give her mind over to other matters while completing the necessary task. Several concerns were battling for supremacy in her thoughts.

Tom had quizzed her last night on Sylvia's current liaison.

"Ask her yourself," she countered. She wasn't going to act as a go-between. Tom had muttered something about taking advantage of someone else's vulnerability. Viv muttered something back about having a bit of backbone. That abruptly put an end to the conversation.

If she weren't feeling awkward herself about Sylvia's current state of being, she might have been more encouraging. The truth was, she knew Sylvia was settling for second best in every area of her life now. She was house sharing with someone for convenience more than anything else, working in a repair shop rather than focusing on her design career; she was burying her inspiration in a rather nondescript shopping mall. Sylvia had passion, talent, and skill, and she was allowing it to go to waste.

Viv was going to have to pull out of the Australian business concerns she had been associated with to concentrate on the London location. It was her golden challis. She had done the hard yards, learnt the business skills along with the design and marketing strategies. Now it was either make or break. She knew she could do it. In some ways, she acknowledged her parents' shortcomings. True, they were self-absorbed. However, Viv and Tom were loved and nurtured. They had known a busy, happy home. Peter and Meg had passed on a great work ethic. She and her brother owed them a lot. It would be wonderful to have Sylvia working alongside her, but she could not contemplate her inclusion in the project unless she regained her sense of wholehearted ambition. It had to come from her.

Viv heard Bibi hang up the phone, unsure as to whom she had been speaking. She left her packing and went to find Bibi.

"Everything okay, Bibi? Who was on the phone?"

"Your mother." Bibi appeared a little agitated, but then her face broke into a smile and she began to giggle.

"Mum? Let's put some coffee on, shall we? She's not still threatening to sue the vicar, is she?"

"No. There was no mention of the vicar. I think maybe she's forgotten about Elvis Presley and his hips!" They both laughed together. Vivi set about making the coffee. "No, it's not about suing the vicar. Meg has another plan under consideration." Bibi sat in a comfortable chair. "It concerns the house."

"The house? You mean their home in Cornwall?" Viv decided on mugs for the coffee.

"No, for this house." Bibi waited for Viv to get the milk from the fridge and pay attention. "This house—the one that I live in and you live in when you're here and that Tom stays in when it suits. The family home. The one we invite people to when we are in the mood. This house."

"Oh." Viv noticed that the smile had left Bibi's lips. "What kind of plan?"

"She wants to turn it into a bed and breakfast."

CHAPTER 25

PERTH, WESTERN AUSTRALIA, TUESDAY

Suzanne accepted Nina's offer of dropping her off wherever she needed to be. "If you would be good enough to take me to my mother's place, Nina? She lives close to the hospital, as it happens. I'll phone Ben from there."

"I'd be happy to, Suzanne." Nina fell silent as she negotiated the exit into heavy traffic.

"I suppose you want me to keep quiet about seeing you."

"You think I'm a cow, don't you?" Nina merged into the traffic. "You'll have to direct me. I can't remember where your mother lives."

"Sorry. Drive on for about five kilometres. And no, I don't think that. I just never understood why you left." Suzanne became more conscious of the pain in her wrist and adjusted the Velcro tag slightly.

"You mean, Ben didn't say anything?"

"You'll need to be in the left lane. No. What did Ben have to do with it?" Suzanne suddenly felt nauseous.

"Look, I should talk to Alan properly before … Oh God. I don't know. I have no right to ask anything of anybody. I know that." Nina changed lanes. "Left on Charter Avenue?"

"Yes. A couple of kilometres, then right onto Westbourne Way."

"Anyway, what about you? Why is life so awful?"

"Because I am a cow—an absolute bloody cow. I've ruined everything. I think if I left, everyone would be much better off." Suzanne closed her eyes. "I feel sick. I need to sleep."

Nina had no idea what to say. She concentrated on looking at the street names as she drove along the tree-lined avenue.

"We're almost there. Look, here's the street. What number?"

"It's thirty-five." Suzanne laid her head on the back of the car seat.

Nina pulled up outside a handsome, well-kept two-storey home.

Suzanne undid her seat belt awkwardly and opened the car door. "Thanks. If you don't tell anyone about me, I won't tell anyone about you."

Nina watched her hobble her way up the pathway to the front door. She was barefoot. Nina wasn't sure what had happened to the Jimmy Choos. Gina answered the door almost immediately, calling out anxiously for Frank. Nina drove away. Maybe she had better forget about the whole thing. Leave well, or ill, alone.

Nina was left feeling ill at ease. Just as she had begun thinking about the possibility of Alan forgiving her, she quite literally bumped into his sister-in-law in bizarre circumstances.

Her dramatic disappearance with no explanation seemed the right thing to do at the time. But it had been unfair. Mostly to Alan, admittedly, but that was just the tip of the iceberg.

Alan had been her first serious boyfriend. She had an aura of vulnerability about her that many men found extraordinarily attractive. She went on occasional dates but was never attracted to anyone in particular. Alan had been older. He didn't hassle her or crowd her. Instead, he wooed her with unexpected romantic gestures. Once, she found an envelope placed in between two bunches of roses at the florist shop in which she worked. She had no inkling as to how it came to be placed there without someone noticing. Inside was a card with a pressed flower on the front. It read as follows:

> *Are roses red?*
> *Are violets blue?*
> *I can't say for sure,*
> *But I know I love you.*

Grandiose gestures didn't feature much in the early days of their courtship. Spontaneity did, however. An unscheduled walk in the park or picnic at the beach delighted her. There was very little spare money. Nina liked there not being much money. Simple living was a necessity, yet it was how she wanted to live anyway. When they married, they resided in a tiny flat, and she loved it. But Alan began to gain a reputation as a competent real estate agent. Money became more readily available. The more money there seemed to be, the more insecure Nina felt.

Alan mistook Nina's perturbation. The more she withdrew, the more he tried to love her. Nina felt she might die from suffocation. The worst thing was, she couldn't say it. Any of it. How could you ask someone not to be successful? How could you get off the merry-go-round?

When her period was late, she panicked. A baby. She wasn't ready for a baby. It would complicate everything. Alan would tell her it would be fantastic. He would assure her that he would be very hands-on. That wasn't it, though. She wasn't sure if she was still in love with Alan. How could she love a baby? A baby would have to come first, another life totally dependent on you to fulfil its needs. Why did anyone want to do that? They would more or less have to focus on making sure there was enough money. Babies used to live in a drawer for the first few months, didn't they?

She had to get away and think, work out her priorities. She could go home to her mother for a bit. Ironically, she hadn't the money for the fare.

William was anxiously awaiting Sylvia's return. She handled all the alterations and repairs admirably. Ruth had filled the gap well, but she was becoming a bit too friendly with Crystal for his liking. Nevertheless, he had to admit that there had been noticeable improvements in Crystal's attitude. He hoped Brenda would forget all about this college placement she felt Crystal deserved. Indeed, Crystal's future, or lack of it, seemed to be taking up a good deal of Brenda's time and energy nowadays. She seemed to have lost some of the interest in the catering ventures that proved lucrative for William. Between the repairs and alterations, dry-cleaning, car hire, chauffeuring, rental, and extras, such as Geoffrey and Martin's discretionary payments, he did very well.

Approaching the dry-cleaners, however, he felt a little apprehensive. Leini, the younger of the two staff members he employed, was talking with a man. Not unusual in itself, apart from the fact that he was behind the counter rather than in front of it. There was no sign of Leini's grandmother.

"Ah, Mr. William." Leini smiled pleasantly. She spoke more than adequate English, unlike her grandmother, who didn't seem to offer as much as a syllable in any language. "I was waiting for you. I was starting to get a bit worried as you not here. I like you to meet my brother, Branislav." William smiled nervously in the direction of Leini's brother. Branislav chose not to reciprocate.

"Hello," Branislav said thickly. He stood confidently behind the counter with his arms crossed in front of him. Heavyset, he appeared almost twice the height and breadth of William. "We not waste your time. I ready to open my restaurant. My sister, I need her for waitress and paperwork. She leave. She want money you owe to her and Shozi."

"M-money?" William stammered. "They are supposed to give me notice. I don't think I owe them—"

"You not pay properly. I know this. I am businessman. They leave now. They want, let us say, five hundred dollars."

William swallowed. "Five …"

"Hundred. Each."

William reddened but moved no closer to the counter.

"You owe more, but they leave now, so that is fair. We go, Leini." Branislav opened the hatch to allow William through. "You get money, please."

William was speechless. He inched his way past Branislav. Shaking, he opened the filing cabinet, retrieved a wad of cash from a yellow envelope in the bottom drawer, and handed it to Branislav meekly. "Do you want to count it?" William enquired.

"No," Branislav answered. "I trust you." And he smiled, revealing almost perfect teeth.

With that, the two of them walked off the premises and made their way to the closest exit, leaving a dumbfounded William staring in their wake.

His world was falling apart. He had lost his dry-cleaning staff quite unceremoniously and been duped out of one thousand dollars to boot. Admittedly, he had underpaid both of them, but they'd seemed grateful for the work. After all, the grandmother couldn't even speak English. Then there was the incident with the car taken, albeit probably for a joyride, but why vandalise it?

William had made the grave mistake of underestimating Rhonda. He wanted a trustworthy soul to clean both his business premises as well as his home. Efficient, reliable and undemanding, she didn't mind doing extra chores such as cleaning out the fridge or tidying the linen cupboard. Having left school at an early age to help care for younger siblings, William presumed a lack of intelligence on her part. But he was wrong. Rhonda cleaned the theatre also. Geoffrey utterly enthralled her.

One of life's "angels," Rhonda could often be found helping out a friend, or even a friend of a friend who needed a lift to the hospital or their cat fed for a week and suchlike. She would help anyone who seemed to be down on their luck or finding it a bit tough. Over time, Rhonda came to mistrust and eventually dislike William. She and Geoffrey would often have a little laugh at William's idiosyncrasies and peccadillos. A few months ago, Geoffrey had confided in Rhonda as to his and Martin's predicament. Naturally enough, she was appalled at William's misuse of information. She labelled his behaviour as blatant blackmail and wanted to alert the police. Geoffrey managed to persuade her that there was more than one way to skin a cat.

Rhonda had access to almost all of William's keys and security codes. The little disclosures between her and Geoffrey were harmless enough as far as she was concerned. Geoffrey and Martin's Egyptian costumes were both legitimate and also a distraction. The police officers were talented actors from the theatre, as were the bogus car hire patrons.

Members of the backstage crew knew their way around mechanical devices and hardware. As Geoffrey would say, "It's all smoke and mirrors, darling."

Ben had been greatly relieved to hear Gina's voice on the phone the night before. She called twice, first to stop Ben and the girls from worrying. Later, having seen Suzanne off to bed with some painkillers, she had filled Ben in on the accident resulting in a sprained wrist and the story about him needing to pay some money into the school office due to the muddle caused by taking one of the staff to the hospital.

"Now then, I've got to go into Jade's school this morning, so I need you to behave like grown-up girls and walk sensibly to your classrooms for me. You can tell your teachers that Mummy hurt her arm and couldn't drive the car. Remember, Grandma will be picking you up this afternoon. You'll stay at Grandma's place until the weekend. Mummy will be there with you. Grandma is looking after you all for a bit." Both Ben and Jade were surprised at how subdued the younger two girls were. Ben supposed having the opportunity to tell some rather dramatic news to the class might well carry enough import for them to be behaving in such an acceptable fashion. And tomorrow, if Suzanne had a support brace on her wrist and the abrasion on her face clearly showing, they would have the chance to embellish the tale further.

Jade went straight to class and left Ben to see the office staff.

"Would I be able to speak to Chaplain Rachel, please?"

The office receptionist explained that she was resting at home.

"Ah, yes. I understand there was some trauma yesterday. I hope all is well." Ben smiled winningly, and the usually somewhat caustic receptionist blushed in spite of herself.

"I need to make a payment of one hundred and sixty dollars. I believe my wife has filled in the paperwork."

Skimming through the payment slips efficiently, the clerk found the relevant item. "It seems to have been paid, Mr. Meadows. She showed him the form and indicated the tick in the "Paid in full" box.

"No, my wife explained to me how in the confusion of getting the young lady to the car and off to the hospital, the payment wasn't made. No fault on your part, I'm sure!" Ben smiled once more and removed his credit card from his wallet.

"Oh no. Naturally. We were all very concerned. I'll fix it now." Ben tapped his card, and she printed up a receipt. "Thank you." The phone rang, requiring her to tear her eyes away from his. Momentarily, she forgot how to answer the telephone. She felt herself blush once more.

Alan was surprised to receive a call from Ben. And he was even more surprised to receive an invitation to dinner that evening. "A boys' night. I'll cook something."

"A boys' night? And you'll cook something?" Alan was incredulous.

"I know. But there'll be no women. We can talk … about things."

"Things?" Alan repeated. "Ben, this better not have anything to do with Delvine, because I—"

"*No!* Absolutely. Look, are you going to be here or not?"

"Okay." Alan became aware of a customer pulling into one of the parking bays. "But don't cook. I'll bring in a curry. Madras? Six o'clock?"

"Six thirty. I need to walk the dog. Thanks."

CHAPTER 26

Opal had shared the dramatic story of her missing, injured mother with her class, and she felt she had gained a fair amount of kudos in the telling. Quite a few hands were raised to ask her questions. Mrs. Bender congratulated her on presenting her news well. She had stood still, spoken clearly, and remembered the facts. Mrs. Bender was pleased that Opal's mum would soon be well again and Grandma was able to be such a help.

It wasn't quite the same for Pearl. Unable to recall the medical term "sprain," she had upgraded it to a broken arm. Ms. Brown felt reasonably confident in amending the exaggeration and then went on to explain to the attentive children the difference between the two conditions. Of course, this resulted in the teacher being the centre of attention, instead of Pearl. Ms. Brown thanked Pearl and directed her to sit down. It was story-writing time. Pearl could write all about it in her book and draw a picture to go with it.

Twenty minutes before the end of the school day, Ms. Brown requested that they all spend a few minutes tidying their drawers, picking up any mess from the floor, and then be sitting on the mat ready to listen to the next thrilling instalment of *Explorer Pete and the Island of Dinosaurs*. The afternoon was warm. Pearl picked up a few stray pieces of litter, threw them into the bin by the open door, and snuck outside.

Ms. Brown finished the chapter as the sound of the siren signalled dismissal time.

"Where is Pearl?" She scanned the group of children nervously. "Has anyone seen Pearl?" Ms. Brown crossed the room to look outside where the bags were. "Lindy and Makesh, would you mind just checking in the toilets for me, please? I think Pearl must be in there. Quickly now." She noticed a well-dressed older woman coming towards the classroom, smiling readily. Probably Pearl's grandmother.

Lindy and Makesh ran back to class eagerly, yelling, "She's not there!" Ms. Brown experienced a terrible sinking feeling in her stomach.

"Good afternoon," said Gina. "I'm collecting Pearl. I decided to come to the door, as it isn't usually me who picks them up."

"Grandma!" Opal had walked to Pearl's classroom. Very sensibly, Gina noted.

"Ah, Opal, isn't it? Could I ask you to dash back to your classroom and see if Pearl is there?" *Please, God,* she thought.

"You mean she isn't here?" Gina's eyes widened. Opal dropped her bag and ran back to her classroom.

"She can't be far away." Leah Brown smiled reassuringly at Gina.

"She'd better not be, Ms. Brown," Gina retorted after scanning the welcome sign on the door. The smile had left her face. "We don't need another missing person!" There was no mirth in her voice.

"Excuse me. Sorry, but Timothy didn't have a new reader this week. Can we change it?"

"Certainly. Let's see." Pleased with the distraction, Leah Brown directed Timothy's mother to the box of readers, located his record card, and found a suitable book. She deliberately began a conversation about how pleased she had been with Timothy's progress, hoping to goodness that Pearl would turn up in the meantime.

A breathless Opal returned, shaking her head. "Oh, Grandma. Where is she?"

"Don't worry, Opal; she can't be far away. Ms. Brown, would you keep searching, please? We'll go to the office." Gina took Opal's hand and marched away to the office building. Her tone had made it abundantly clear that she was not happy with Ms. Brown.

As soon as they arrived at the office, Opal bemoaned tearfully, "We've lost Pearl! First we lost my mum—and now we've lost Pearl!"

The secretary behind the desk was dumbstruck, not entirely sure what was meant by the term "lost" in this particular case.

The principal came through from her own office immediately. "What's the problem?"

Gina explained the situation.

"Mr. Danvers, could you come here, please?" Mr. Danvers was a young smart-looking deputy. "We need to search for a missing student. Usual routine. I can assure you that this is not an infrequent occurrence. Every so often, a child gets it into his or her head that they will go and explore or talk to a friend about something. They are never far away. Seeing as you have Opal with you, it might be better if you stay here."

Gina was struggling to hold herself together. Should she phone Ben? Making a call would at least make her feel she was doing something.

"What?" Ben was amazed. "That's ridiculous. Not you, of course, Gina. I mean, she can't be missing." He wanted to add, "What the hell is wrong with my bloody family? I just want normality, for God's sake."

"The principal and the deputy are searching. Don't come here. I'm sure I'll be calling you back in a few minutes."

"Fifteen. Call me in fifteen minutes." He wouldn't be at all surprised if Pearl were deliberately seeking attention. Things happened, though, didn't they—accidents or worse? He grabbed his keys in spite of himself. He had to be there.

Pearl had been discovered around the back of the canteen, squeezed between the back wall of the building and the boundary fence. Lodging herself in, she was ready to stay there for a while. Everyone would be so pleased to find her. After about ten minutes, she got bored. The siren sounded, and she suddenly felt she might get into big trouble with her grandma. That was when she spotted a massive spiderweb a little above her head. She squirmed out of reach, but her hair brushed against it, causing the owner of the trap to move towards her. She panicked and began to scream. Two waiting parents heard her cries of alarm. It took a while to ascertain the location of the screams. By the time she had been dragged free of her hiding place, she was sobbing uncontrollably. The women were unable to discover which class was hers.

"Pearl!" It was Mr. Danvers. He used a firm, controlled voice. "What on earth are you doing here? Everyone is looking for you!" He didn't sound as if he was going to give her the kind of welcome she had anticipated.

"I want Mummy!" she wailed at the top of her voice.

Alan was waiting to pick up his madras curry. He was still somewhat bemused at Ben's invitation, not having been briefed as to why Suzanne and the girls were at her mother's. As he and Sylvia had agreed, there had been no phone calls, just a safe arrival message. Sylvia and Viv had shared a taxi and were "sorting out a few things." Alan didn't know what that meant, but he was almost relieved not to see Sylvia anyway. He still couldn't get his head around what to do.

"Come on in," said Ben. It was a little after six thirty. "I'm glad you've brought food. I've only just got back. More drama!" Ben filled Alan in on Pearl's escapade. They spoke a little about the business and what was in the news. Alan was intrigued as to what Ben might have cooked. Ben confessed that he probably would have ended up with takeout. The conversation seemed to falter a little.

"You know, it sounds so trite, I suppose. But not knowing what had happened to Suzanne and then this afternoon with the scare about Pearl—I tell you." Ben shook his head. "If anything happened to any of them, I couldn't bear it. I've been a jerk."

"You think?" Alan was prepared to let Ben know precisely what he thought. He should have done it before now.

"I know, I know. I'm a bastard, and I'm ashamed. Totally ashamed."

"Suzanne adores you."

"Yeah, but she doesn't feel loved back. I know. I want to put things right. But I don't know where to start. Let's finish off this food, shall we?" They shared the remains between them.

"And with you, Alan, I haven't always done the right thing. I'm sorry."

"No. You're hard on yourself as far as that goes. You practically saved me."

"It's not that simple, mate. Before we go any further, I've got to tell you a few things." Ben poured more wine. "You'll need this," he said. "You can stay here, if you like."

CHAPTER 27

Sylvia and Vivienne were subdued in the cab.

"Bibi was sad to see us go, I think. Of course, the situation wasn't helped by my extremely insensitive mother prattling on about this ludicrous idea of a bed and breakfast."

"You'll stick to your guns, then?"

"Absolutely! First and foremost, the house belongs to Bibi. Why would she want to share her home with itinerant guests? It doesn't bear consideration. How selfish is my mother to contemplate it? Secondly, Tom and I both use it. Okay, not full time, but it suits both our jobs and lifestyles to have it available to us. It's also a nice way to keep watch over Bibi. Mum and Dad are free to use it whenever they want to. No way can she turn it into a bed and breakfast. I must admit that I was pleased to see Bibi show such determination. She's caved in for most of her life. Tom can be diplomatic and strong too. I'm sure he'll make sure Mother doesn't get her own way."

Mentioning Tom's name caused Viv to broach another matter. "You'll be pleased to see Alan, I suppose?"

"In all honesty, Viv, no. I'm glad I didn't arrange for him to pick me up from the airport. I'm feeling sick at the thought of facing him." Sylvia rummaged in her handbag for a lip balm and applied it generously.

"What do you mean?" Vivienne prompted.

157

"Alan's a lovely man. A good man. And he has been devastated by his wife leaving. I know that, and if I leave as well, then ..."

Viv delved into her handbag and furnished them each with a butter-menthol lozenge.

"Thank you. He deserves better than me, doesn't he? And so do I. We should both be with someone who makes us happy. And it's not just that, Viv. I'm sorry. You're my best friend, but I am so bloody jealous!"

"Of me?"

"Yes. You've done so much with your life. I'm working in a shitty little shopping mall for some bloke who thinks he's God's answer to I don't know what. Just what is the difference between Crystal and me? Nothing. Except for a few years, that's what. I don't think I can do this anymore. I don't. I've appreciated your willingness to take some of my makeover designs for your market stall. But I want to try to make it—even if I starve trying."

Sylvia had initially been pleased with Viv's offer of an alternate place to stay. However, as the evening wore on, she felt more and more uncomfortable about the whole thing.

"I've got to tell him, haven't I? I know it's hard. But I can't be Nina. I shouldn't even try to be Nina. Alan's not happy. I'm not happy." Sylvia slumped despondently onto the trundle bed she would be using. Viv occupied one room in a house share when she was in Perth. "But what if he—I don't know—completely flips? He'd be left on his own again. I could phone. No, it would be awful by phone. But then, if I go there and then leave, is that worse?"

Vivienne filled the kettle from the tap over the small basin. "Could you meet somewhere neutral, for coffee, perhaps?"

Sylvia's phone alerted her to a message. "Oh, it's Alan."

He'd written, "Glad you've landed safely. I'm staying over at Ben's tonight. Long story. See you tomorrow."

"Well, that doesn't much sound as if he's desperate for my company, does it?" Sylvia decided that the delivery of bad news could wait until tomorrow. She wasn't quite sure if she was placated or annoyed.

"Tomorrow will be quite a day, then. Dump Alan and hand in my notice. No partner. No job. No place to live."

"Sylvia, stop this. You've got some decisions to make. You're the only one who can make them." Vivienne took a notepad and pen from a drawer. She handed them to Sylvia. "Write down your options—options requiring a *yes* or *no* answer. Have a good night's sleep. In the morning, you respond to the list. Then you do what you need to do to make things happen."

"How come you're always so together?"

"I'll ignore that. Start your list or you'll be losing an always-so-together friend."

Sylvia doodled on the top of the paper for a while and then began writing:

> *Do I want to live with Alan?*
> *Do I want to work in a repair shop?*
> *Do I want a career?*
> *Do I want to live in Australia?*

"I already know the answers to all these questions."

"Good. But leave it till the morning to work out what you must do. Let's watch something stupid on TV for half an hour.

As usual, Matthew had left for his shift. An hour later, Rachel began having quite severe pains. Determined not to panic, she made a note of the time. When the contractions were twenty minutes apart, she would phone him. He would return home and take her to the hospital. She'd packed her bag and was ready to go. By the time she had the third contraction, her resolve had weakened. She wanted Matthew. Grabbing her phone as soon as the pain settled, she rang his number. Hearing the familiar ringtone via her phone, it slowly dawned on her that the ringing was coming from close quarters. It was in the entry, on recharge.

"Goddammit! He's forgotten his phone! Of all the days!" She hung up and tried to think clearly.

Delvine's phone rang as she was getting into her car. "Hi, Rachel."

"Dee, Matthew's left his phone behind. I can't ring him. I'm sure I'm ... Oh, Dee, I want Matthew. I'm scared! I can't do this on my own. I can't think what to do."

"Okay. Try to take the breaths as they taught you. I'll be there soon. You've got the number of Matthew's unit. If not, you should be able to get it from general police enquiries, I should think."

"Yes, yes, of course. Obvious. Sorry ..."

"Don't be daft. I'm on my way. You ring the man!"

Mathew was filling out paperwork in anticipation of the evening's expected outcome. He was due to attend a nightclub in the city at about ten. Bandit would be assisting with drug searches. Matt had a strange feeling when he left home earlier that this might be the night. He would be sure to ring home before leaving for the potential bust.

"Matthew." A tall, lanky officer came through from the office. "Apparently, your wife has been trying to contact you. Want to give her a ring?"

"Thanks, Sergeant." Matt felt around in his pocket for his phone. Realisation slowly dawned. He remembered plugging the phone in to recharge. He didn't remember picking it up before he left home. "Oh no. Oh God. Sarge, can I use the office phone? Emergency?" He didn't wait for an answer but went directly to the phone in the office. "Pick up, pick up, pick ... Rachel!"

"Matt, please come home. Please. I'm ... *Oooh.*"

"I'm coming. I'm coming. I'm there." He slammed down the phone. "Sorry, Sarge." He dashed from the premises. Bandit followed without being invited. Matthew dropped his keys, found them, and dropped them again. Stopping, he placed two hands firmly on the roof of the car. "This is not good." He addressed himself silently, *Matthew Kirk, you are a police officer. Act like one.* He opened the car door calmly, sat inside with Bandit, and turned on the engine.

Matthew's sergeant couldn't help but smile. He had three under his belt and a fourth on the way. Nothing seemed to cause quite the same reaction. Babies knew how to make an entrance.

James Frederick Kirk was welcomed into this world at 5:23 a.m. on Thursday, October 15, 2018. "Would that be after Captain James Kirk, by any chance? Are we Trekkie fans?" asked the midwife.

"No," said Matthew as he took the baby into his arms. He smiled at Rachel. "The surname is a given, and we like the name James. However, there is a degree of historical respect there."

The midwife looked blank. "Don't tell us," she said playfully. "Hey, Noreen, any ideas? James Frederick Kirk—not Starship *Enterprise* apparently, but a historical link."

"James Frederick Kirk." Let me think for a minute. James Frederick … Oh, the initials! JFK? President Kennedy?"

"Got it." Matthew glowed proudly.

"Whatever the link is," commented Rachel, "it's a thousand times better than Fatso!"

Ben and Alan talked well into the night. One bottle of red became two. Disclosures flowed along with the wine. There were anecdotes shared about their childhood years. They had experienced hard-working, no-nonsense loving parents.

"Ya know, you probably won't believe this, but I've been envious of you." Ben took another generous gulp of red.

"You're right," Alan snorted. "I don't believe you."

"No, hear me out, mate. When Nina first came on the scene, you two had this incredible joy in each other. Suzanne was a good catch, I'll admit. But I honestly thought I was a good catch. But I wanted what you had, until it all went wrong. I could see you both going under, and I thought, *Well, that's what happens.* But then Nina came to see me one night. And this is one of the things I've never told you about."

"Nina came to see you? Why? About what?"

"You really want to hear this?"

"Of course, I want to bloody hear it! Hear what?"

"Remember, mate—water under the bridge. I did what I thought was, you know, right. At the time."

"Tell me!" Alan thumped his glass on the table.

"Nina said she thought she was pregnant and had to get away. She was going to her sister and would let you know when she got there, but I wasn't to let on about anything. She was a mess. So I gave her money and took her to the airport."

Alan was stunned. Nina had left a brief note, saying she had to go away for a while and she would contact him soon. Nothing was Alan's fault. She just had to get away.

"I did plan on telling you, but you completely fell apart, and I thought it would just make it worse. Then the more time went on, the harder it got. When you started to get better, I was scared that if I told you about the baby and her not wanting you to know where she was, it might send you over the edge."

Alan drained his glass. "You said *one of the things.* Bloody hell, Ben."

"You won't believe this either ..."

"Stop fucking telling me what I'll believe, will you?"

"Thing is, I don't know if I believe it myself."

"*What is it?*"

"Suzanne is adamant that the person she collided with, the person who took her to her mother's after the accident, was Nina."

CHAPTER 28

PERTH, WESTERN AUSTRALIA, THURSDAY

For Sylvia and Vivienne, the late hours of Wednesday evening became the early hours of Thursday morning.

After sleeping for a while, they whispered like high school boarders. They returned to the topic of Sylvia's list.

> *No, I don't want to stay with Alan. It's unfair to both of us.*
> *No, I don't want to spend the rest of my working life in a repair shop.*
> *Yes, I definitely want a career.*
> *No, as much as I like Australia, it's not where I should be right now.*

"So ... what to do? There is never a good time. But I guess it should be today. Hand in my notice, also today. I no longer consider myself a small-time seamstress. I am a dress designer. I'm good at it. I don't know when or why the dream stopped. I need to be in London. I need to get my work seen and worn. I need money to get there and some extra to live on, a place to stay and some design contacts. I can stay with Mum, I'm sure. It will be good for us. Contacts. Well, I'm looking at one at least, aren't I, Viv? Money problem. There has to be a way. I've no jewellery, only a little in savings. Hey, a car! I have a car. Dare I ask

Alan? He can refuse in which case I suppose I take it somewhere else." Sylvia checked her phone. "Five minutes to three.

"Six o'clock."

"No," said Viv. "It's three o'clock."

"No, I mean, I start my new life at six o clock. No turning back. I've got to do this, Viv."

"Wonderful," Vivienne drawled. "I'm sleepy again now. See you at six, then." She rolled over and went back to sleep.

William was putting on a brave face. The vandalism to the car, although not permanently damaged, made him feel very uneasy about hiring it out again. It would take a while to get the dry-cleaning business running efficiently once more. He would have to employ more staff. The previous two were a lucky find. He had been able to negotiate terms in his favour because of their quite urgent need for work. He wondered if a couple of Crystal's friends might be amenable.

Ah. There was Ruth, quietly efficient and spurring Crystal on to work. They appeared to be sharing a joke. "Good morning, ladies!"

"Good morning, William. You've just missed Geoffrey. He was up with the lark, and he imparted some wonderful news to Crystal. Actually, why don't you phone your mum, Crystal? There are no customers yet. Oh, sorry, William. Do you mind if Crystal makes a call to Brenda?"

"Of course not." The mention of Geoffrey rang alarm bells. He was featuring far too often in William's life recently. "What's the good news?"

"Geoffrey has found me a place in Theodore College." Crystal located the number on her phone as she explained excitedly to William. "I can't believe it. I have to attend an interview and take an original work along, but Geoffrey says he's sure I'll get in.

"Hello, Mum. You will never guess what!" Crystal took the phone through to the rear of the store. William had never seen Crystal so animated, he thought ruefully.

"Yes, that is wonderful news. I'm not sure I've heard of Theodore College, Ruth."

"In Melbourne! How exciting is that?"

Ruth was demonstrating a rather unseemly level of enthusiasm, William thought.

"Melbourne? Heavens, it's as well Sylvia will be returning to work on Monday, then!" He felt a sense of relief. Brenda wouldn't let Crystal go to Melbourne. Goodness knows she could get into all sorts of trouble.

"Oh, and look at who's here! Sylvia! You look wonderful." Ruth quickly came through the partitioned door and hugged Sylvia warmly. "We must have coffee and you can fill me in on everything."

"Absolutely." Sylvia broke away from Ruth and turned towards William a little awkwardly. "If we could have a little chat, please, William?"

"Of course, Sylvia. I'm all yours." William led the way through to the back of the store. Sylvia was probably after a pay increase, he thought. Well, he had the ready excuse of his recent tales of woe to ward off any immediate changes. Crystal brushed past her.

"Hello, Sylvia!" Sylvia had to look twice. She hardly recognised Crystal. She was smartly dressed, with no gum and a smile that lit up her face beguilingly.

"Crystal, assist Ruth with the usual morning tasks, please. Sylvia and I have some things to discuss."

"William, thank you so much for accommodating my need to go to London at such short notice. It was much appreciated. I'll get straight to the point. I've realised that London is where I should be. I want to make a go of it on my own. Designing, you know. I need to hand in my notice, effective immediately."

William was dumbfounded. His shock gave way to a chuckle. "Of course. I've always admired your designs, Sylvia, but it's a difficult world to break into, you know." He smiled indulgently. "I suggest you retain your position here while you build up some contacts."

"Thank you, William, but no. I already have contacts through Vivienne. She is closing down everything to do with her Australian business interests to concentrate on a new venture in London. I'm working on designs that will form part of her clothing outlet and market stall. Actually, an upmarket stall is a better way of describing it! I'm talking about the real deal, William. I have to do this for me. I'm sure you understand."

William could think of nothing to say. He just nodded his head and sat down rather slowly on a nearby chair.

"There should be a little bit of paperwork, I suppose—tax and so on? Here is my letter of resignation. Can we deal with it now? I've got a few things to organise today."

While William accessed all the documents he needed and printed them up for her to sign, he related his recent misfortunes. Sylvia made sympathetic noises but didn't seem overly interested.

"Have you included the super payments, William?"

"I'm doing that now. Dammit, this thing is so slow this morning." Everyone seemed preoccupied with their own agendas nowadays. Sylvia would be sorely missed, but there was no way he was going to tell her that.

Finally, everything was sorted out. "Well, goodbye then, Sylvia. All the best." Sylvia didn't fail to pick up the note of sarcasm.

"Thank you, William. Ruth, I'll ring you about coffee. Crystal, you too, if you'd like."

William could go and replace his own flaming zippers. Appropriate really, seeing as he was a self-serving prick.

Despite the wine and the late night, Ben and Alan were awake at six and surprisingly coherent with each other. Both seemed aware that the barrier separating them had begun to crumble. They made eggs and toast.

"I've got some things to say," Ben began.

"Me too," said Alan. "But you can start." He got cutlery out of the drawer for both of them and sat up at the breakfast bar.

"I know I've got to try to put things right with Suzanne. Splitting up my family isn't an option—it's a cop-out. I'm better than that. I'm not sure on the how yet, but the resolve is there, on my part at least. The other thing is that it's time *we*, I mean you and I, should become business partners. What do you think?"

"Are you serious? You're willing to put your trust in me?"

"I'm dead serious. And going by the last few years, I'd say you're the most trustworthy one of the two of us! We should be proper, legit partners. It's the right thing to do."

"I've been soul-searching, as it happens. You said you were jealous of our relationship, Nina's and mine. And I've always thought about it being she who ran away and why she did that to me. But really, I have to take the blame for her getting to such a point of desperation. If she couldn't share with me her feeling of unhappiness or even tell me there might be a baby—I think there probably wasn't—to be honest, then I have to acknowledge failure on my part. It takes two, don't they say? And by the way, the second-hand car yard does extremely well!"

"So that's a yes, then?"

"Sure is, partner. Good eggs. Coffee?"

Alan went home to shower and change. He felt like a new man. The two brothers were very different, but that didn't mean they couldn't work together effectively or become closer.

He was fifteen minutes late arriving at the yard. Robert and Delvine were both behind the counter, talking companionably. He would cook dinner for himself and Sylvia tonight, and then they had to have a serious talk. It was not going to be easy. However, a working day awaited. Alan saw a car drive into the yard. *Early bird,* he thought. Hang on—that car was familiar, as was the face of the driver. Sylvia!

"I'll take this one," Alan said to Robert and Delvine. Oh God, he hadn't prepared for any rushes of affection. Had her heart grown fonder with absence? Would he have to burst her bubble here in the yard? Or was she mad at him? Somehow picked up on something? Would there be a showdown?

Sylvia parked the car and alighted. Alan approached the vehicle.

"Sylvia!"

"Alan!"

"What? How?"

"You first," they both echoed, and began to laugh.

Alan pointed at her, indicating he was ready to listen. Silently he willed her not to smother him in kisses and proclaim undying love.

"Would you consider buying my car, Alan?"

That was unexpected. "Buy your car? Do you want to upgrade?"

"No. I want …" She looked directly into Alan's eyes. "To be honest, I need money for an airfare—and a bit more besides. If you can see your way clear to helping me, I'd be enormously grateful."

"Sylvia, do you want to come through to the office?"

"No. No, thanks. I'm fine. It's just difficult to explain." She shifted her bag from one shoulder to another. "Could we sit in the car?" Not waiting for an answer, Sylvia sat in the driver's seat. Alan took a detour and sat on the passenger side.

"Are you in trouble? Of course I'll help. Selling the car is a bit drastic." He laughed, hoping to lift the mood. Sylvia began laughing too. "God, Alan, I knew this wouldn't be easy. You are such a beautiful man." She laughed again. "Okay. Please just listen. I realised while I was away that I had in fact run away to Australia. It was meant to be a short stay alongside Vivienne, but somehow it turned into a buried existence. I was running away from a strained relationship with my mother. I was running away from a bizarre relationship with my father. I was running away from my designer dream because I wasn't dynamic like Vivienne and I somehow thought it would never become a reality. And I was somehow running away from myself. Weird, eh? But I know now that I should be in London, making it happen. I know I can do it. Vivienne's got all the contacts. She's concentrating fully on an outlet in London. And I've just got to be there." She looked at Alan, waiting for a response.

"Are you saying that you are leaving me, Sylvia? You want me to purchase your car so you can buy a ticket to London and swan off to pursue your dream?"

Sylvia looked away. "I'll try another dealer, then, shall I?"

"Oh, no, Sylvia. No, you won't. You will sit there and hear what I have to say. Okay?"

Sylvia went cold. She wondered if he might secretly be armed. She was glad the car door had remained open. *Make no sudden movements,* she warned herself.

Alan rested both hands on the dashboard, closed his eyes, and began to laugh. His laughs turned to guffaws. In the end, he was holding on to his ribs, trying to stop himself from further hilarity. "Sylvia, Sylvia. No offence, but seriously, that is the best news I have heard in weeks. You have no idea. Really."

"What do you mean? Best news? What the hell is wrong with you?"

"Nothing," he said. "Nothing at all. But you will have to listen. It's my turn."

CHAPTER 29

PERTH, WESTERN AUSTRALIA, ONE WEEK LATER

"Mr. Ben Meadows has asked if he could see you this morning, Robert, at ten thirty in his office."

"Mr. Big? Sorry. Okay. Do you know what it's about?"

"I do know, Robert, that you'd better cease with the Mr. Big jokes or you'll find yourself using the terms indiscriminately."

Alan was smiling; nonetheless, Robert felt somewhat chastened. He had been aware of a change in Alan over the last week. It was as if he'd grown an extra inch or something.

"I'm not in trouble, am I?"

"As far as I am aware, you're not, Robert. Don't be late, though. He's got his reasons for asking to see you."

Ben and Alan had made no announcements regarding the partnership on which they were about to embark. They planned on waiting until all the paperwork was signed and dealt with, and then they would invite all the staff to drinks in Ben's office and inform everyone of the changes.

His immediate boss, Nev, had advised Schubert to come to work presentable and smartly dressed on Friday. He was to bring workshop clothes with him so that he could resume his usual car maintenance tasks in the afternoon. Raymond and Aileen had taken Schubert under their collective wings, as it were. They felt he had lots of potential. Raymond had arranged a meeting with Alan for Schubert at ten thirty.

Suzanne had more or less fully recovered from her fall, but Gina insisted on driving her daughter and granddaughters to and from school to give Suzanne's wrist a chance to strengthen. Suzanne felt she owed the school staff some thanks and apologies for Pearl's unruly behaviour. Mrs. Bender assured her that she had no need to remonstrate with herself, while at the same time handing her a card advertising the family counselling services of a friend of her daughter's. Mrs. Bender gently patted Suzanne's wrist. It was still enveloped in a protective sleeve.

"Give it a go, dear. I'm sure it will prove worthwhile," she advised encouragingly. "We all need help with life's pressures from time to time."

Changes had already begun in their household, however. Suzanne's mother had unearthed a compendium of board games when she was having a clear-out. Ben grabbed the set without hesitation. The two younger girls were to play one of the board games each afternoon from Monday to Thursday, supervised by Jade, who would act as referee should it be necessary. If they played cooperatively, without fighting, they would earn points towards a technology session on Friday. Jade was to be rewarded with dance lessons for her assistance with the younger girls and helping Suzanne with dinner. Suzanne had discovered a collaborative weekly sewing group; they worked on costumes for the musical.

Ben suggested that he and Suzanne both clear away after the evening meal each night and talk to each other about things both meaningful and trivial. Ben had also promised to babysit one evening a fortnight to enable Suzanne to attend a drawing class. Neither of them had ever mentioned the diary and the scrawled pictures Ben had found. One evening he came home with an easel and materials from an art shop, which she arranged in a well-lit recess by the front door full, in full view of anyone who entered the house. Suzanne had confessed her gambling weakness to Ben. In turn, Ben acknowledged his regret at his philandering ways. They were on a new road.

William's usual visit with Brenda on Sunday had provided more disappointment. Rather than finding Crystal in a sulk because Brenda would not allow her to go to Melbourne and take up the college placement, he found the two of them excitedly discussing plans for a joint move. Brenda had relations there, apparently. (Brenda had relations everywhere.) A cousin had offered for them to stay with her. She would enjoy the company.

"Presumably, this is just while Crystal settles." William took a seat at the table.

"No. I want to give Crystal the best opportunity I can. Be there for her, you know. The course is for two years, and then she will have to establish herself somewhere."

"You mean that this is more or less permanent?" William was shocked. "What about the house?" He managed to stop short of saying "What about me?"

"I'm renting out the house. Geoffrey and Martin are very keen on it." Brenda and Crystal carried the plates to the table.

"But Geoffrey and Martin rent from me!"

"Yes, but they want to get into gardening, of all things! Anyway, that's a nice flat. You'll have no trouble finding a tenant."

"When is this all going to happen? I've lost Sylvia. I'm going to lose Crystal. My world is falling apart, Brenda. Goddammit! What have I done to deserve all this?" William pushed his plate away from him. "I can't eat, Brenda. It's all so horrible."

"Don't be so dramatic, William. You'll soon get yourself back on your own two feet. And I shall be mortally offended if you don't eat that meal. I'm not used to my food being rejected."

William had managed to talk Ruth into working for a little longer. Crystal and Brenda would stay until just before Christmas. Then he would sell the two fancy cars and just settle for a small one. There didn't seem any point in hanging on to anything much. He wasn't going to sit behind that repair counter himself.

The latter end of the week saw William cleaning his two good cars. Funnily enough, cleaning quality cars gave him a good deal of pleasure—especially once he saw them gleaming. His mind wandered for a moment as he contemplated the more affluent suburbs situated not far from his residence. Would they pay to have a smart, well-spoken valet obviously cleaning their expensive vehicles at the front of their property? Once a week or fortnight? Would those same residents also pay for a chauffeur to be their designated driver when they wanted to eat out with friends or go to the theatre? Maybe he could do valet and chauffeur deals? A slightly different angle to his previous car business. He would be the valet, the chauffeur, the "uniform." It could prove a more straightforward but perhaps equally profitable enterprise.

Glowing, Robert returned from his interview. As he came in the door, he was a little surprised to see a smart and happy-looking Schubert making his exit. They acknowledged each other.

"Thank you, Mr. Meadows!" Robert was grinning from ear to ear. That was all down to you, wasn't it?"

"Mr. Ben Meadows and I discussed it. And you have proved yourself since you've been here, so well done, Robert."

"I start in the new-car division a week from Monday. Does that leave you short-staffed?"

"You passed Schubert earlier. He's going to begin a traineeship with me. Delvine will be showing him the ropes concerning record-keeping and so on. At least I think she will," Alan said a little mysteriously. "She asked for time off to go to an appointment at eleven. She's due back in about half an hour."

Delvine walked in through the door at a few minutes to one, sandwich in hand. "Thank you, Mr. Meadows. Might I have a word with you, please?" Alan and Robert exchanged looks. Had she found another job? They would miss her.

"I'll check on that Honda that came in earlier," Robert said as he went outside.

"Take a seat around here, Delvine." Alan indicated to the chairs behind the desk.

"Mr. Meadows, I hope you know how much I've appreciated the job I have here."

Alan nodded. He would be sad to see her go. But people moved on. A while ago, he would have worried about her and Ben, but he now knew that she wouldn't entertain the idea of a liaison—and Ben seemed to be a changed man.

"You've heard me talk about Rachel and Matthew and their baby boy, James?"

"Yes, occasionally, if I recall." They both laughed.

"I know. Not everyone loves babies. Well, anyway. They are keen for me to stay with them and help out for a while, and that would suit me, because …"

"Because?" Alan urged.

"Because I want to go to Uni."

"Oh! That's wonderful, Delvine."

"I want to do nursing. I'd love to work with babies. But it would be good to have some work as well. Not full time. I wondered if there could be any way we could negotiate."

"Definitely. Perfect timing. Come back to me tomorrow with a proposition for about, say, twenty hours? All my staff are beaming at me today!"

Sylvia and Vivienne were seated in the departure lounge. She kept passing admiring glances over her newly acquired travel luggage. Alan had been very generous. He had given her money for the car and the airfare, plus some more to help get her set up, however she might need it.

They heard the call for their flight come through and took out their phones to turn them off. Just at that moment, Vivienne's phone alerted her to a message:

> *Hi, Viv. Hope this message gets to you. I'll meet you at the airport. Can't wait to see you both. Counting the hours …*
>
> *Tom X*

Viv handed her phone to Sylvia. "I think this is a message for you," she said, smiling. "Counting the hours? Well, who'd have thought?"

CHAPTER 30

PERTH, WESTERN AUSTRALIA, THE WEEKEND.

Alan sent an uncomplicated email to Nina, inviting her to his place sometime over the weekend. He found himself waiting for her at around six o'clock on Saturday. She said she remembered where the house was and requested that he not prepare food. Her car drew up just about on time.

He was careful to keep his distance when she got out of the car. She looked as she had always looked - quite lovely.

"Hello again. Thank you for the invitation. I've brought eggs and grated cheese with me. I can make us an omelette, if you'd like. But what's this?" Nina looked beyond him and smiled. "I love those little old camper vans. Sometimes people do them up, don't they? It's yours, I suppose."

"Not quite yet. I'm still deciding what to do with it. Tell me, if you had one of these, what would you do with it?" Alan expected her to say she would lose herself every weekend and tell no one where she was.

"Easy. I'd paint flowers all over it and use it as a drive-by sales van. I reckon the classy suburbs would go for it. Don't you think?"

"It's worth thinking about at least." They fell silent.

"Alan, I'm sorry for leaving the way I did. I hurt you badly, and I have big regrets. I involved Ben in it too, and I shouldn't have. I thought there was a baby. There wasn't, but I didn't even tell you."

"It was as much my fault. I wasn't prepared to listen because I somehow thought I would lose you if we tried to work out what the problem was. I am truly, truly sorry."

"I understand that you've got a life with someone else. But it is good to talk properly—to forgive each other if we can."

"No. There's no one else, Nina. Sylvia has left for London of her own accord. She wants to pursue a design career. I think she's done the right thing." They fell silent.

"So is the omelette offer still on the cards? We could eat, and then I thought you might like—" Alan dug his hand into his jeans pocket — "to take a little test drive?" He jangled the keys enthusiastically.

"You drive first," Nina said. "I can't cope with too much excitement in one day. I'll get the eggs and cheese."

Alan waited for her to collect a small bag from her car. Walking into the house together, both looked over their shoulders and linked hands. They realised they were offering each other the most precious of gifts. Both were prepared to give, and take, a second chance.

CPSIA information can be obtained
at www.ICGtesting.com
Printed in the USA
BVHW031415311019
562603BV00004B/25/P